"What if we

Mick couldn't be serious.

"Until Beatie's in a better place. She should have answers by Christmas, and after that, we can tell them we're just friends."

As tempted as Sadie was to avoid hurting Beatie, she wasn't sure she could agree to this. "It feels like fibbing... But this made her happy. And she's probably so scared right now."

"Would you be willing, if it didn't mean lying?" Mick's expression was impossible to read.

Her words turned to gurgles in her throat. "What?"

"Maybe we should just date. Our grand romance can be over by the New Year."

"If our relationship has a predetermined expiration date, then it's not real."

"We'd be two people spending time together. No one else has to know there's no romance involved."

"And we like to hang out together anyway." She couldn't think straight, but she couldn't deny she wanted to make Beatie smile. "Maybe...pretending through December wouldn't be so bad."

"So, we're doing this?"

"We're doing this."

Susanne Dietze began writing love stories in high school, casting her friends in the starring roles. Today, she's an award-winning, RWA RITA® Award–nominated author who's seen her work on the ECPA and *Publishers Weekly* bestseller lists for inspirational fiction. Married to a pastor and the mom of two, Susanne lives in California and enjoys fancy-schmancy tea parties, the beach and curling up on the couch with a costume drama. To learn more, say hi or sign up for her newsletter, visit her website, www.susannedietze.com.

Books by Susanne Dietze

Love Inspired

Home to Foxtail

Mountain Homecoming
Her Pretend Holiday Beau

Widow's Peak Creek

A Future for His Twins
Seeking Sanctuary
A Small-Town Christmas Challenge
A Need to Protect
The Secret Between Them

Love Inspired Historical

The Reluctant Guardian
A Mother for His Family

Visit the Author Profile page at LoveInspired.com.

HER PRETEND HOLIDAY BEAU

SUSANNE DIETZE

If you purchased this book without a cover you should be aware that this book is stolen property. It was reported as "unsold and destroyed" to the publisher, and neither the author nor the publisher has received any payment for this "stripped book."

INSPIRATIONAL ROMANCE

Recycling programs for this product may not exist in your area.

ISBN-13: 978-1-335-62123-8

Her Pretend Holiday Beau

Copyright © 2025 by Susanne Dietze

All rights reserved. No part of this book may be used or reproduced in any manner whatsoever without written permission.

Without limiting the author's and publisher's exclusive rights, any unauthorized use of this publication to train generative artificial intelligence (AI) technologies is expressly prohibited.

This is a work of fiction. Names, characters, places and incidents are either the product of the author's imagination or are used fictitiously. Any resemblance to actual persons, living or dead, businesses, companies, events or locales is entirely coincidental.

For questions and comments about the quality of this book, please contact us at CustomerService@Harlequin.com.

® is a trademark of Harlequin Enterprises ULC.

Love Inspired
22 Adelaide St. West, 41st Floor
Toronto, Ontario M5H 4E3, Canada
www.LoveInspired.com

Printed in Lithuania

MIX
Paper | Supporting responsible forestry
FSC® C021394

O lord, thou hast searched me, and known me.

I will praise thee; for I am fearfully and wonderfully made: marvelous are thy works; and that my soul knoweth right well.
—*Psalm* 139:1,14

For my mother, Virginia Copeland, a teacher,
a warrior, and beloved mom and grandma.

And in memory of our beloved Ruby,
who kept me company while I wrote many a story,
including this one. You were a gift of God to our family,
and we miss you, fluffy girl.

Chapter One

Sadie Dalton registered the blur darting across the two-lane mountain road and slammed on the brakes. Her minivan squealed to a stop and she lurched forward, peering into the misty fog. Was the fox gone?

At least, she thought it was a fox. Bushy tail. Pointy ears. Silvery fur on its back and reddish-brown markings. It had to be a gray fox. Thankfully, she hadn't registered any sensation of impact with the animal.

There was, however, a crash behind her.

Not on the road—few cars were out and about so early on this damp November morning—but in the rear of her silver minivan.

The slosh and splat of her flower buckets tipping, the thunk of the cardboard box falling over, and the splinter of glass as the slate-blue vases tumbled out of it and broke.

"Thanks, Mr. Fox—or Mrs. Fox," she muttered. "You picked a great time to cross the road."

But it was her fault she was in this pickle, not the fox's. She had been a florist all her adult life. She knew better than to gather supplies at the last minute. Yet here she was, working under a ticking clock, and she didn't have enough time to turn around and make the hour-long drive from Goldenrod in California's Cuyamaca Mountains back to the San Diego flower market where she'd snagged them.

She also knew how to brace boxes and flower buckets better than she had, but she blamed her errors on feeling rushed. She would never have been in this position if she hadn't been under so much pressure this past week.

Although, if she were being honest, she'd been stressed and off-balance for almost three years now.

She resumed driving, wincing at the clinking of glass shards, but she was determined to trust God's provision. In the ten years she had been following Him, He had never forgotten or abandoned her, had He?

Nope. Not like…

Never mind. She had to focus on the task at hand, not the pains of the past.

Sadie took a slow, calming breath of the botanical-fresh scents coming from the rear of the minivan. What did she have back in her little floral workshop to work with? *Think positive. But think fast.*

Within a minute, she was approaching the familiar sign with the silhouette of a bushy-tailed fox, welcoming her to Foxtail Farm. Sadie drove through the empty visitor parking lot toward the rear of the house-size wooden farmstand building where her floral-design workshop was located.

Except she couldn't park in front of it. Not when a dented, faded-red horse trailer was already parked in the loading zone.

It wasn't the trailer her cousin Thatcher used at the ranch next door. Nor did it belong to her brother-in-law Wyatt, who was preparing to start a therapy ranch. Therefore, whoever it belonged to had no business parking here. Hadn't they read the sign?

Foxtail Farm Employees Only.

Bad enough if she didn't need the spot, but she did. And she was in an all-fired hurry.

She parked at an angle behind the empty trailer, stomped out of her minivan and slammed the door behind her. "Excuse me." Her vinegar-toned words carried on swirls of vapor in the chilly autumn air. "You need to move. Now."

A shaggy yellow dog with pointy ears bounded out from the other side of the trailer.

Sadie's ire melted as she bent to greet the mixed breed, whose black nose snuffled around the hem of her work jeans and the tops of her battered tennis shoes. "What a surprise, Fly, girl. What's with this trailer? Where's your person, anyway?"

A person who, as a doctor of veterinary medicine, might not be a Foxtail employee, but if anyone could park in her loading zone and get away with it, he could.

Sadie rose and strode around the trailer. Sure enough, the familiar gray truck that had towed the trailer here belonged to Fly's owner, Mick Larson, but the man himself was nowhere in sight. He couldn't have gone far, since Fly was here. The dog had been Mick's shadow since he rescued her five years ago.

Oh well. With a mess in the rear of the minivan, Sadie didn't have time to hunt Mick down.

Please help me, God. You know how much today's contract means to me.

Before she reached her minivan, the sound of boots on the damp asphalt drew her around. Mick appeared from behind the farmstand, shoving back the waves of dark hair curling onto his forehead. His charcoal utility jacket couldn't disguise the breadth of his strong shoulders, nor could the dark stubble shadowing his square jaw hide the dimple that she secretly yearned to touch.

Just once.

But they were friends, and that wasn't the sort of thing friends did. Instead, she smiled back. "You're up and at 'em early."

"So are you. Where've you been?"

"The flower market. What's all this?"

He gestured at the horse trailer. "Surprise!"

A surprise could mean a lot of things. Most likely, Mick meant something along the lines of *Aren't you surprised to see me here, at this hour?*

But she decided to tease him anyway.

"A surprise for me? On Best Friends Day?" Her hand went to her thick brown flannel jacket, somewhere in the region of her heart. "Aw, you shouldn't have bought me a horse trailer, Mick, but thanks."

"It's Best Friends Day?" His smile melted into an abashed O.

She had no idea when Best Friends Day was. And she and Mick had never labeled themselves as anything more than regular old friends. Everyone they knew had pushed them for years to start dating—a hazard of being close friends to folks with matchmaking tendencies.

Sadie shoved all thoughts of the town's nosy Nellies out of her head. "I'm pulling your leg, silly. You gestured at the trailer and said *surprise* like you were giving me something."

Always up for their good-natured ribbing, he laughed. "Trust me, you do not want this thing. It belongs to the clinic, and it should have been replaced ten years ago. Maybe twenty. But you know how Coggins is."

The senior partner at Goldenrod Veterinary Associates, Leonard Coggins was a caring and proficient vet, but a notable miser, much to Mick's lament as his junior partner. Mick was often frustrated by Dr. Coggins's refusal to update the clinic's technology or replace worn-out items—like this trailer, apparently.

Sadie wasn't an expert on these sorts of things, but the trailer did appear to be held together by zip ties, duct tape and possibly prayer. "I've never seen this before."

"We rarely use it, but today is a special circumstance. Wanna meet Gidget?"

"There's something in the trailer?" It had looked empty. Sadie shuffled back to get a better angle at the open side windows, but no horse gazed back at her.

"Here." Mick unlatched the trailer gate and lowered it to reveal the cutest little pinto Sadie had seen in her thirty-one years of life.

"A pony!"

"Miniature horse, actually."

Now that he mentioned it, Gidget didn't quite look like a pony. She was built like a horse, but her proportions were shrunk down into an adorable mini package. "She's beautiful."

"Beautiful and smart." Mick clambered into the trailer. "She's a trained service animal."

"And she is in a time of need, I take it?" Mick often fostered animals because the animal shelter was always full. He was always good at finding them the perfect homes, too, but a miniature horse was a first.

"Sadly, yeah. She helped a woman with severe vertigo in Borrego Springs, but unfortunately, the owner is moving to be with family and her daughter-in-law had concerns about Gidget's size. The family found the horse a new home, but that arrangement fell through last night. They didn't know what to do, so they started calling veterinary clinics. It was after hours, so as you can imagine, they couldn't find assistance until they tried us. The clinic's answering service knows to call me if there's an emergency or situation like this."

"You weren't already in bed, I hope."

"It was after midnight, so I was, but I managed to get a nap in before I had to leave at four to go get her."

Sadie's hand fell still on Gidget's neck. "Phone calls in the middle of the night can be distressing."

"But this wasn't bad news." His eyes went soft. "That makes all the difference."

She knew exactly what he was referring to. A middle-of-the-night call had alerted her to her dad's unexpected death almost three years ago. As difficult as it was to lose him, the unpleasant surprises had continued after the funeral, when she, her sisters, Natalie and Dove, and their cousin Thatcher learned they had inherited Foxtail Farm—with a tangle of strings attached.

According to the will, the four of them were required to live and work at Foxtail Farm for five years, changing nothing in the way the "U-Pick" apple orchard, farmstand, bakery or adjacent ranch were run. Otherwise, all four of the Daltons would lose their inheritances, the property would be sold and their employees would lose their jobs.

What choice could Sadie have made but to quit her job at Goldenrod Floral Design, the store that would have been hers to run someday had her father's death not pulled her away from it?

Now she spent her days selling the gifts, gourmet foods, and fruits and vegetables the farmstand had sold for years, with the addition of a few of her floral arrangements, since the farmstand also sold seasonal flowers and greenery. To help scratch her designer itch, she'd started advertising her availability for side projects a while ago, and the word was slowly spreading around town that Sadie sold arrangements that were equal in quality and cheaper in price than her former employer.

But growth was slow because the fact remained that the farmstand wasn't a floral-design shop. Sadie missed being a full-time florist, but she had gladly sacrificed her career to help her family.

Hopefully, she could at least salvage the flowers in the back of the van for today's client.

Her face must have looked unhappy, because Mick touched her arm. "Wow, that was insensitive of me. I shouldn't have brought up your dad's passing. I'm sorry."

"Never apologize for bringing up my dad. It's not like I don't think of him, anyway. I was just thinking how one phone call in the middle of the night changed the direction of my life." She wove her fingers into Gidget's fluffy mane. "I don't think Gidget will necessarily alter the course of yours, though."

"Probably not, but finding her a home will be a bit of a challenge. Normally, I would make arrangements with the training group where she came from, but the owner fell out with them and insisted I can't use them—she added it to the paper we both signed when I took Gidget. I'll make some calls during normal business hours, but in the meantime, she needs somewhere to go."

Sadie well knew there was no room for Gidget at the overcrowded animal shelter. She might not be more than thirty inches at the withers, but she required more room to move than the shelter allowed. Gidget wasn't the kind of animal a lot of people could accommodate.

But some of Sadie's relatives could. "Fortunately, I know a guy with a stable. Two guys, actually."

"Me too." He was close friends with her cousin Thatcher, and Wyatt, her new brother-in-law, happened to be Mick's cousin. Both men lived on Foxtail property, and both owned horses. "Wyatt said Gidget could bunk with the Flower Girls."

Wyatt's mares were all named for blooms, much to the approval of Sadie's flower-loving heart. She stepped back so Mick could lead Gidget out of the trailer. "Is Wyatt meeting you?"

"Nah. He's feeling better today, but the kids are still pretty cranky, so I told him to stay at home."

Wyatt, like everyone else in Sadie's family, had been down with the flu for a full week. Sadie appreciated her new brother-in-law's commitment to the orphaned girls he and her sister Natalie were in the process of adopting. Granted, she was sensitive about the subject of hands-on dads since her own father had been so unreliable.

But why think about something so unpleasant when there was an adorable little horse right here? Once Gidget was on the ground, Sadie returned to rubbing her neck and back. "She doesn't even come up to my waist. I love her so much, Mick."

"Want to come with us to the stable? Get her settled?"

"I wish, but I only have a few hours to put together eight centerpieces for a luncheon at the Women's Auxiliary today."

His brow furrowed. "That's not like you. You usually complete arrangements a day ahead."

"I try, but with everyone down with the flu last week, I'm behind from doing elements of their jobs." And not necessarily well either. Sadie was a florist, not an office manager like Natalie, proficient in spreadsheets and schedules. Not a baker like Dove or a rancher like Thatcher, but she had done her best to cover the most important of their tasks while they were ill.

To the point where she had not been able to do elements of her job until the last minute. Her vanload of flowers was a case in point.

Mick's blue eyes went soft. "I don't have to be at the clinic for a while. After Gidget gets squared away, I can help you, if you tell me what to do."

Normally, she'd decline—but today? "I'll take you up on it because of the fox."

"The what?"

"I'll explain later." Then, with regret, she bid Gidget goodbye and strode back to the minivan.

Lord, give me grace to handle whatever I'm about to find. She opened the rear liftgate.

Oh boy. The panda anemones were untouched, and the dusty miller, eryngium and Silver Brunia had survived well, but the cardboard box of cream roses was dented.

Worse, though, were the four shattered vases. She had only purchased two extras in case of a break, so she would have to replace all the vases for the sake of uniformity. She didn't have enough milk glass or clear glass vases of appropriate size in her workshop, and the rest of her available stock was the wrong color, since most of her upcoming sales would be harvest themed in shades of red, gold and orange. Today's client had requested slate blue.

She racked her brain for a moment.

Good thing Mick had offered to stick around. If she were going to pull this off, she would need his help.

With Fly at his side, Mick knocked on the door to Sadie's workshop, then let himself into the square room at the rear of the farmstand. Generally, he would be instantly met with the botanical scents of greenery and blooms, but this morning what hit him was the unmistakable earthy smell of pumpkin.

"Thanks for coming." Sadie's warm brown eyes crinkled as she smiled. She had traded her flannel jacket for a black apron and bound her straight blond hair into a twisty bun at her nape. She stood at her large worktable in the room's center, surrounded by tools, buckets of flowers and greenery, damp cardboard and plastic packaging, and several squat grayish-blue pumpkins that almost looked fake, but the orange flesh Sadie scooped from one proved it was a real vegetable.

Or fruit. He could never remember how pumpkins were classified. Fauna was his thing, not flora.

"Hey." He held up his phone, revealing the quick online search he'd executed while walking over from the stable. "There really is a Best Friends Day. In June. I thought you made the whole thing up."

"I made up that it was *today*, but I'm not surprised it's a legitimate thing." With a squelch and a splat, she dumped pumpkin innards atop a large sheet of brown paper. "There are official days to celebrate just about everything. Sisters. Coffee. Reading."

"How about veterinarians?" He glanced at Fly, who settled near one of the heater floor vents—a perfect spot to curl up on a damp November morning.

"There must be. Haven't you received flowers for it?"

"I'm a dude. Who's going to send me flowers?"

Smiling, she rolled her eyes. "I meant at the clinic."

"I don't know. Maybe? I never noticed." He found a mug, selected a single-serve coffee pod and pushed the button on her coffee maker.

"This is a tragedy." She resumed scooping. "What's the point of having a friend who's a florist if you never get any flowers? One of these days, when you least expect it, I'll send you something—"

"Totally not necessary."

"—and on Veterinarian Appreciation Day, whenever it is, I'll create an animal-themed arrangement for the clinic. Foxtails, tiger lilies, birds-of-paradise, and snapdragons, which are also called dog flowers, so don't give me a hard time about including blooms named for mythical beasts."

"Dragons are totally real." He pretended to be affronted as the coffee maker sputtered to a stop. "Komodo dragons, anyway."

Her smile widened. "That was dangerously close to a dad joke, Mick."

"You love dad jokes."

"And I'm not ashamed to admit it—unlike you, afraid to admit you secretly might want to receive flowers."

"You found me out. All these years, my heart has ached at the loss." He smiled at her over the brim of his cup just before he took a long pull of the hot coffee.

He loved how they shared the same sense of humor. When they'd met as teenagers one summer, they had clicked in a way he had never experienced with anyone else. Theirs was a rare and cherished friendship.

Others might not understand, but he and Sadie did. That was all that mattered.

And that was why he was here. "Enough kidding around. How can I help?"

"I'm going to use these Blue Doll pumpkins as vases. Would you be willing to scoop out the guts so I can prep the flowers?"

"I'm all yours." He set down his mug and shrugged out of his jacket. "I haven't carved a pumpkin in years, though."

"You won't be carving, exactly. Just cleaning them out. First, cut the tops off, using this stencil so you know how big of a hole to cut." She gestured at a paper circle and a felt-tip pen.

"Got it." He glanced at the plants on the table, a mix of blue and cream flowers and muted greenery. "These are going to look great."

"I hope the client likes them, because she requested these colors, but I hadn't planned on using pumpkins. I hope she doesn't think they're too, I don't know…harvest-y." Her narrow shoulders shrugged as she carried the hollow pumpkin to the sink.

"Pumpkins make them seasonal, yes, but they definitely don't look like a Thanksgiving cornucopia, if that's what you mean." He got to work with the stencil. "I've never seen gray-blue pumpkins before."

"Yes, you have. These are from the display in front of the farmstand."

"No, the display is orange and yellow." The sound of running water, followed by a faint whiff of bleach, filled the room while he worked. "I helped you set it up. There was corn involved."

"That was for October." She swiped out the pumpkin with a towel. "I switched it out November first for Thanksgiving."

Seeing as how it was now the twenty-first, he must have walked past the new display at least a dozen times now, but he wasn't good at noticing that sort of thing. She'd never minded, though, and her faint smile told him she was more amused than irritated. "I'm sure it looks awesome."

She returned to the worktable. "Hopefully, these centerpieces look awesome too. I would love for this order to go well."

His gut ached for her even as he was in awe of her, working so hard to thrive after her life had endured a twist like her dad's strange will requiring her to live and work at Foxtail for five years.

Thankfully, he had never had to set aside his dreams like that. His memories of helping Grandpa Hank treat sick and injured animals were the most meaningful of his childhood. When his grandpa asked him to promise to stay in Goldenrod and continue his veterinary partnership with Leonard Coggins, it was easy to say yes.

Sadie's *yes* to her family came at a price, however. She'd sacrificed her career trajectory because she was a person of integrity and character.

And if anyone deserved good things, it was Sadie.

"Your client will love these so much that word will spread. You'll be barraged with so many Thanksgiving orders you'll have to turn people away." One last scrape of the orange flesh, and this pumpkin was cleaned out. He reached for another. "Your business will grow. I'm praying for that every day."

"Thanks, Mick." She carried his pumpkin to the sink. "I'm praying for you too. Neither of us is exactly delighted with the current state of our careers."

She had a point. Goldenrod Veterinary Clinic had its issues, but thinking about it now would only frustrate him. "Nothing's perfect, though."

"Hopefully, these centerpieces come close to it." She dried the pumpkin with a towel. "At least I have another job on the books. Blair Bronson's wedding in two weeks. She's coming in this afternoon to make her final selections."

He knew next to nothing about weddings, but this was good for Sadie. "Tell me more about it."

They chatted until he finished with the last pumpkin. In that time, Sadie had donned nitrile gloves and started stripping leaves from stems. Her approving glance took in the pumpkins, and she smiled at him. "Thanks for helping. You saved my bacon, cleaning out the pumpkins for me."

"Mmm, bacon. Now I want a BLT."

"I'll treat you to one next time we're at Trixi's Diner. That's the least I can do for your help."

"That's not how friendship works. But are you sure I can't do anything more?"

"Not a thing."

He was due at the clinic, anyway. He pulled his keys from his jeans pocket and jingled them to awaken Fly from her snooze. Once his dog was up on all fours, stretching and yawning, he waved at Sadie. "I'll be back later to check on Gidget. Maybe I'll see you then."

"Oh, I'd love to go with you to visit her. She's so cute. Thanks again, Mick." She didn't look up when he left, concentrating on her project. He appreciated her dedication to her work. It was one of the things they had in common, like their faith, despite having grown up in families that didn't attend church.

Whistling, he returned to the truck. It took a few minutes to drive to the vet clinic and unhitch the trailer, but before long, he and Fly entered the building through the back door. Judging by the barking in the first exam room, Dr. Coggins was busy with a large dog—was it the Smiths' malamute?

Mick ducked into his office, intending to change into scrubs and a white coat, but he came up short at the sight of Glenda, the fifty-something receptionist who had worked here for decades, planted in front of his desk. She was generally as warm and fuzzy as the teddy-bear sweater she wore over cat-patterned scrubs, but when challenged she was a force, and the glare she turned on Mick now could melt steel.

The reason for her bad mood sat in the spare chair in Mick's office. Wade Gibbons, a slender, balding fellow in his late sixties, was one of the wealthiest men in town, and perhaps the most mysterious. Not because he carried an air of intrigue, but because he never talked about himself. Mick knew him only from church; he'd never visited the clinic with a pet. Had something changed? A quick glance failed to reveal an animal with him.

"This gentleman doesn't have an appointment, Dr. Larson, and he insisted on waiting in your office instead of the lobby." Glenda's pink lips pinched together.

"I'm allergic to cats, and the one in the waiting room set me off." Wade tugged a tissue from his coat pocket and dabbed his red nose. "Do you mind, Mick? This won't take long."

"Not at all." Mick offered the receptionist an apologetic smile. "Thanks, Glenda."

"That cat's up next when you're finished." Glenda blew out a puff of annoyance on her way out of his office, not even pausing to pet Fly like she usually did.

As Fly settled into her bed in the corner of the office, Mick set down his workbag. "How can I help you, Wade?"

"I have a proposition." Wade's hooded eyes glinted behind his silver-framed glasses. "Are you familiar with living nativities?"

"Christmas pageants, like the kids do at church?"

"Not quite." Wade's thin lips twitched. "I mean a walk-through experience, where visitors stroll through sets where actors in biblical costumes tell the story of the first Christmas. Isaiah tells of the coming Messiah. Next, the Romans call for a census, and so on, through the birth of Jesus and the visit from the Magi."

"Sounds impressive. The sort of thing that would bless the community, for sure."

"I'm glad you think so, because I want Goldenrod to have

one. A free one-night-only outdoor event on the Saturday before Christmas. And for it to feel authentic, there must be animals present. Sheep. Camels. Chickens, perhaps—although chickens roost when the sun goes down, don't they? Never mind the chickens."

A big undertaking, with a lot of moving parts. But why was Wade here? "Did you need my opinion on the animal aspect?"

"Yes, but what I want most of all is for you to run it."

Wade's excited grin was a strong counterpoint to the sinking feeling in Mick's stomach. "Me?"

"You'll have complete creative control," Wade continued. "Where to hold it, whom to cast, what the sets should look like. If you check your email, you'll find that I just sent you instructions, links to videos of past living nativities in other towns for inspiration and reference, as well as a script and a prepaid debit card to cover all the expenses—but I wish to remain anonymous."

Money hadn't entered Mick's mind, and it was honestly the last reason he had to say no. He hoped his smile was apologetic enough not to hurt Wade's feelings. "I appreciate you thinking of me, but running productions, dramatic or otherwise, isn't…my thing."

Wade's faint brows drew together. "You've organized plenty of pet-adoption events in partnership with the animal shelter."

"After months of planning." Mick hated the crestfallen look on Wade's face. "Tell you what. I'll help on the committee. With you at the head, things will be sure to go how you want them to—"

"I can't do this myself." Wade's smile melted. "I'm leaving town this afternoon and won't be back until the day of the nativity."

Mick shook his head, but Wade held up his hand. "The nativity is a gift for my neighbor, Cassandra. She came to faith at a living nativity in her youth but hasn't experienced one since. I want to give her one as a present."

Quite a gift. "I can help you search for one online." Mick tapped his computer keyboard to wake up the machine. "I'm sure there's got to be one in the vicinity."

"She has cancer, Mick. In a few hours, she's leaving for an experimental treatment at the Mayo Clinic. I'm going with her so I can visit her each day she is in the hospital. But should this be her final Christmas, I want her to have a living nativity, here in town, so she won't have to travel far to experience it."

Mick couldn't help but be touched and, at the same time, slightly envious. Generous, sacrificial love was not something Mick had much experience with, not the way he had been raised. And certainly not in his few romantic relationships.

But that didn't mean he couldn't recognize a sweet gesture, and as generous as this one was, Mick couldn't help. "I could never do a project like this as well as it deserves. I have work. Church. Volunteering at the shelter."

"Ah, yes. The animal shelter." Wade pulled a folded check from his pocket. "That is why, in exchange for you taking charge, I will fund the expansion to the shelter you told me you hoped for when last we chatted." He thrust the check toward Mick's hand.

Mick was afraid to take it, but he didn't want to hurt Wade's feelings, so he opened it. And gulped. It was postdated to the date Wade proposed for the nativity, and the dollar amount would cover an expansion, all right—and then some.

But how could he say yes to heading up such a huge event? He was busy. Out of his element.

But how could he say no? A nativity would bless a sick woman, the community and, once the shelter was bigger, a host of animals for years to come.

"I'll let you treat that cat now." Wade moved toward the door, leaving the check in Mick's hand. "Text me your decision, will you?"

Mick shut his eyes. He needed to pray for guidance, but all he could think about was why Wade had chosen him. This was the sort of thing Sadie could do in her sleep, not Mick.

Sadie. The knot in his stomach eased.

But first things first. He reached for his white coat and headed toward the cat in the waiting room.

Chapter Two

Sadie loved November at Foxtail Farm. The harvest might be over, but the trees were still beautiful, their red and gold leaves rustling in the crisp mountain air, which was scented with pine, grasses and the occasional whiff of spices from the bakery. The mountains were draped in green and gold, and the critters who dwelled on the wooded property were busy gathering stores for winter. Despite the lack of "U-Pick" apples now that harvest was over, visitors still came by for Dove's pies and cider doughnuts, as well as pumpkins and seasonal gifts from the farmstand, especially with Thanksgiving just days away.

Autumn was not to be rushed through on the way to the winter holidays, in Sadie's opinion. But at this moment, she set aside thoughts of the arrangements she'd placed in blue pumpkins this morning and shifted her thoughts toward Christmas. Christmas weddings, in particular.

"Mistletoe." She enunciated each syllable as she wrote the word on her legal pad. "Did you want them fashioned into kissing balls, or should I leave them as simple sprigs for the reception hall?"

"Oh, kissing balls for sure. At least three. There should be lots of romance at this party." Her bridal client, Blair Bronson, shifted on the bench across the picnic table. Sitting outdoors had been Blair's choice, but with Sadie's assistant manager, Elena Morales, running the register, she was free to leave the farmstand. After the misty morning, it was good to feel the warmth of the sun on her shoulders while she and Blair studied photos of suggested ideas on Sadie's tablet.

Lots of mistletoe balls, Sadie wrote, adding an *XO* after.

"Now that the reception flowers are done, let's talk about my bouquet." Blair shoved a loose chunk of dark hair behind her ear. "White roses. Some sort of greenery to make it festive. And something different. Isn't there a flower called Christmas rose? Would that look good?"

Giving an affirmative hum, Sadie tapped on her tablet to bring up an image of white flowers composed of five petals and yellow filament-like segments in the center. "*Helleborus niger*. They aren't really roses, but there's a legend about them. A little girl in Bethlehem wept because she didn't have anything to offer Baby Jesus, but her tears caused these flowers to grow, and she gave them to Him."

"That story makes them even better. Let's add some to my bouquet." Then Blair's gaze shifted over the tablet. "You just got an email alert. It says *important* in all caps. You can check it now, if you want. I need to text my mom, anyway. I can never remember if she's allergic to lilies or gardenias, and I should find out before we plan the other arrangements."

Grateful for Blair's understanding, Sadie tapped her tablet screen. The email was from an old friend, Ruth. As teens, they'd worked together at Goldenrod Floral Design, but Ruth had moved on and was now a florist in Los Angeles.

The email from Ruth was short.

Remember when you wanted to do this two years ago, but then couldn't? Well, he's offering it again in January. You should apply!

Beneath Ruth's brief message was a forwarded email advertising a month-long program—an internship, of sorts—with a florist whose work she had seen in magazines.

"Who's that?" Blair leaned across the table, pointing one red fingernail at the photo at the bottom of the email.

"Alessio Adami. He's an artist with flowers."

"So are you, Sadie."

"That's kind of you to say." But she had a lot to learn. Almost three years ago, she had been accepted to attend the same training course, but she'd had to cancel when her dad died.

She'd had to cancel everything, in fact. Including the opportunity offered by the owner of Goldenrod Floral Designs to run the shop when she retired, because Sadie had to work at Foxtail Farm.

But in just over two years, when the terms of her dad's will were completed, Sadie could once again pursue her dream to own her own floral shop. To that end, it might not hurt to sharpen her skills. The internship would certainly look good on her résumé. And January was slow at the farmstand, so her family could do without her for a month. She wouldn't be gone long enough to go against the part of her dad's will that required her to live permanently on Foxtail property.

Sadie closed the email tab. She shouldn't be thinking about this when she had genuine work in front of her right now. "What did you hear from your mom?"

"Lilies make her sneeze."

"No lilies, then."

Blair's selections for the other arrangements were made quickly, all in festive reds and whites with greenery that would be perfect for a Christmas-themed wedding on the first Saturday of December. As Sadie finished up jotting down notes, Blair unscrewed the top of her water bottle. "Now that the flowers are all done, I can turn to everything else on my to-do list, like the catering."

"That sounds like a fun task." Sadie scribbled down a reminder to order #3 ribbon. "Who's doing the food?"

"Morris's. It was a no-brainer since Easton is one of the groomsmen."

The pencil went still in Sadie's hand.

"Ooh," Blair continued. "Maybe you can do his wedding flowers, too, if they haven't contracted anyone yet."

"He's engaged, then? To Hallie?" It was hard to say her name.

"Yup. The wedding is next summer... Sadie, you look upset. You're over Easton, aren't you?"

"A hundred percent over him. It was four years ago."

"Ancient history. You two didn't work out. It was no one's fault."

That wasn't quite how Sadie saw it. No relationship was perfect, of course, but Sadie hadn't seen the breakup coming. Especially since, mere days before he told her they didn't have a future, he had sworn that he and his now-fiancée were just friends.

Then he'd asked Sadie what style of engagement ring she wanted.

She'd forgiven him, and Easton Morris wasn't worth another minute of lost sleep or indigestion. She wasn't thrilled at the prospect of seeing him again, but she could handle it.

"It's all good," she assured Blair.

Blair's perfectly plucked eyebrows were still squished in concern, though. "Why don't you bring a date to the wedding? It'll be way more fun for you."

"Thanks, but I'll be fine." Neither of her sisters knew Blair well enough to be invited, but Sadie wouldn't be friendless at the wedding. Foxtail Farm's sixty-something orchard managers, Dutch and Beatie Underhill, were related to Blair and planned to attend.

"Just bring someone." Blair's eyes sparked. "Better yet, let me find you a date."

"You need a date, Sadie dear?" A feminine voice sounded surprised as twin shadows appeared over Sadie's shoulder. "How exciting."

Great. Beatie and Dutch had appeared as if drawn from her thoughts, and they had obviously overheard that embarrassing snippet of conversation.

Sadie turned to greet the pair, who were more like family than coworkers to her and her sisters. Dutch, with his rangy build and long, graying sideburns, looked down at her with curious blue eyes, while Beatie, her faded red hair hanging straight down her back, clutched her hands over the chest of her red Foxtail sweatshirt as she grinned with unabashed excitement.

Sadie had never met a more relentless pair of matchmakers.

"Nope." She forced a smile. "I don't need a date."

"Yes, she does," Blair said over Sadie's head. "So she doesn't feel uncomfortable around Easton Morris."

"I won't feel uncomfortable." But Sadie was sure feeling that way right now.

Beatie fisted her hands at the waistband of her faded jeans. "If that so-and-so is there, you could use support."

"He busted your heart six ways to Sunday," Dutch added.

And apparently, the whole world thought she wasn't over it because she hadn't been on a date since then. "I'm fine."

"Who wants *fine* when you could be amazing? Sit with us, you two," Blair insisted, gesturing for Beatie and Dutch to join them. "Let's brainstorm candidates."

"Don't mind if we do." Beatie reached out with both hands to grab the picnic table, but she missed, slipping forward. Her hip hit the table's side and knocked her backward onto the wet grass.

Sadie hopped to her feet, but Dutch was faster, helping his wife to her feet. "You all right, hon?"

"Yes, just clumsy. I forgot to look before I put my weight down." Beatie chuckled, easing onto the bench. "So, what eligible bachelors are you thinking about, Blair? A churchgoer, for certain."

Sadie eyed Beatie, relieved she hadn't been hurt. Not even her pride seemed wounded, which was something Sadie admired. Beatie wasn't the sort to let a misstep ruin her day.

Sadie wanted to be more like that.

But that didn't mean Sadie was okay with this topic of conversation. It set her jaw on edge, but it also dredged up feelings, ancient ones, that would swallow her whole if she let them.

It was like they believed Easton hadn't just broken her heart—he'd ruined any promise of future happiness for her too.

She already knew she wasn't as pretty as either of her sisters. Or as smart as the super-organized firstborn, Natalie, or as bubbly as Dove, the baby of the family. Every boy—then man—she had ever been interested in had friend-zoned her because they liked one of her sisters better.

Except for Easton.

And Mick, a zillion years ago, but that was an adolescent crush. He hadn't reciprocated, but at least he hadn't pursued Natalie or Dove. And thankfully, he'd never figured it out.

Nevertheless, she felt like an ugly duckling among swans. Her friends were motivated by care, not cruelty, so she prayed for patience. "You all are sweet, but—"

"What about Silas?" Dutch threw out the name as if Sadie hadn't said a word. "He's a looker, Beatie says."

"And he goes to church," Beatie added, "but he's a Foxtail employee. It might be inappropriate."

Not to mention his and Sadie's limited conversations revolved around irrigation and apple varietals. They had as much spark as a rained-on matchbook. "Dating Silas would be improper. In fact, this whole conversation is—"

"The new dentist in town didn't wear a wedding ring when I got my teeth cleaned on Tuesday," Beatie interrupted. "Next week when I get my cavity filled, I'll ask him if he'd like to take you out."

"Please don't do that." Sadie's chest was tightening up to the point of pain. She was sure the dentist was a nice man, but she had met him, and he and Easton looked similar enough to be cousins. "I don't want—"

"To get set up with a stranger? I totally understand." Blair patted Sadie's clenched fist. "Why don't you just go out with Mick already?"

Not this again. "We're just friends. No more."

"We tried getting both of them to see sense for years, Blair," Dutch admitted. "He's thirty-three. High time he married, and Sadie's perfect for him. But nothin' doin'. They must repulse each other somehow."

"We don't... That's not..." Sadie's shoulders sagged with relief as Mick's truck pulled into the parking lot. "Speaking of Mick, I see his truck. He's stabling a miniature horse with Wyatt's mares, and I told him I'd help." She gathered her tablet and notepad. "If you think of anything else about the flowers, Blair, shoot me a text."

"Sure, but I'm not giving up on finding someone for you to bring to the wedding." Blair grinned.

"There's no need." She had been trying to say that for a while now. "I've got it covered."

That stopped their lips flapping.

"You do?" Beatie stared in amazement. "You have a fella? Why didn't you say so?"

That wasn't what Sadie had meant. She was trying to convey that she didn't need a date to feel fulfilled or secure around Easton. But it must have sounded as if she already had an escort lined up, because Dutch high-fived Blair, and Beatie—oh my, were those tears of happiness?

There was nothing for it. It would be easier to find her own date than correct their misunderstanding, especially when it seemed to mean that much to Beatie.

"Who is he?" Beatie clutched her hands to her chest.

"Um…it's a surprise." To all of them, even Sadie. "I'd better go help Mick."

Muttering under her breath, Sadie hurried to the parking lot. Mick was already out of his truck, heading her way.

As soon as they were six feet apart, she puffed out a breath. "Boy, am I glad to see you."

His thick brows knit. "What's wrong? The pumpkin centerpieces didn't go over well?"

Wow, Lord, how quickly I forgot Your provision. I'm sorry. She couldn't have executed or delivered that order earlier today without His help. Or Mick's. She should have thanked him first thing. "No—they loved them. Your help this morning made all the difference, and I'm grateful."

"My pleasure, but something's bothering you. Spill it."

She bit her lip. Mick didn't need to hear about her petty problems. But…

She needed a man. And Mick was one. Obviously.

And he was as easy to be around as he was on the eyes,

not that it mattered. But everything about Mick was simple, comfortable, stress-free.

But she couldn't ask him.

Could she?

"Mick, I was wondering—"

Her words faltered when she looked up at him. His concerned gaze focused on her, but his blue eyes looked tired, and a muscle twitched along his set, square jaw.

Her trifling troubles flew away on the breeze. "Something's bothering you too. Is it Gidget? You can't find a place for her?"

"Not yet, no, but that's not it. Truth is, I could use a favor."

"Anything, Mick. You know that."

She would have stopped there, but when his gaze flickered away in a moment of uncharacteristic apprehension, she couldn't help but give in to the need to reassure him. Without a second thought, she reached out and enveloped his solid frame in her arms.

It wasn't a romantic hug, of course, but when his arms shifted from beneath hers and hugged her back?

It went from feeling like she was clasping a sturdy, strong redwood tree to something she had never experienced with Mick before. This time, she was surrounded by the sage scent of his clothes. And his warmth. Who knew the top of her head fit just right under his chin? Her forehead rested against his neck, and she was aware of the strong beat of his pulse against her skin—

She leaped out of his arms as if she were on fire.

The strangest thought flitted through Mick's brain as Sadie shifted out of his arms—that while her hug was brief, he didn't want to let go.

Which was utterly, completely weird. If and when he and Sadie hugged, it was limited to a side-hug, a pat the shoulder-type thing. But now he wouldn't have minded more of the comfort Sadie's hug provided.

Her friendship knew no bounds, did it? Well, maybe it would, once she heard why he was here.

"Do you know what a living nativity is, as opposed to a Christmas pageant?"

"I think so, but I've never been to one. Have you?"

"Nope, which makes the idea of me running one even more ridiculous. Get a load of this." As they strolled around the farmstand onto the path toward Wyatt's stable, he filled her in on Wade's unusual request.

"A donkey isn't hard to find. Elena has one, Clover."

"I knew Elena had horses, but this is the first I've heard of Clover." But that wasn't unusual since she would probably be treated by one of the large-animal vets nearby. Mick helped them out on occasion, but other than minor issues with his family's horses, he didn't provide care for too many large animals. "That's great."

"I doubt we'll find a camel, though." She shoved her hands in her coat pockets as they passed the last row of yellow-leafed apple trees. "Jimmy Sprock has llamas you could use instead."

"He does, but I actually know a camel."

"That's handy. But Mick?" Her smile widened. "Is this the part where you ask me to help you run the whole thing?"

She knew him too well. "Well, you do owe me for scooping out those pumpkins this morning."

"I thought I owed you a BLT." She laughed, a sound he loved. It made him feel happy. "Fine. We'll call it even after the nativity. But we should form a committee. This is too big of an event to handle ourselves."

Smart. "There's one more thing, though. I need an outdoor venue so visitors can walk through 'Bethlehem,' past sets that are large enough to accommodate the animals and actors. I could ask Uncle Gary and Aunt Jillian to host it at their ranch, but honestly, the first thing I thought of when Wade left was you."

"Me?"

"Foxtail, I mean." They entered the acreage where Wyatt had recently built the stable and paddocks. His six mares explored the fenced green meadow, but Gidget was right where Mick had left her, nibbling grass in her own pen. "You've got a parking lot and a lot of undeveloped land. Would your family consider letting me use a patch of the property?"

"Of course we will. I'll officially ask them, but you know they'll all agree. It's for the community, and it spreads the Good News of the Christmas story."

"Having an event like this on your land is a huge undertaking, though. With no compensation for the farm."

"You know we can't do anything new to bring in income according to my dad's will, anyway, so it's no problem." Sadie reached through the paddock rail to greet the miniature horse. "Gidget, how was your day?"

Mick wanted to know the answer to that himself. He let himself in through the gate and approached Gidget, who appeared calm and content. He wished he could say the same for his own mental state.

"How can we pull this off in just four weeks?"

"I don't know," Sadie said. "But we've got this, Mick."

She looked so sure of herself—boots planted on the lowest rung of the paddock fence, blond ponytail hung over her shoulder, confident smile on her lips. She looked…cute.

He wasn't unaware of Sadie's charms, but he would never

pursue anything beyond friendship with her, for her sake as much as his. She was too good a friend, which reminded him.

"When I got here, there was something on your mind. I sort of derailed that conversation." He ambled toward her. "I want to be there for you the way you're there for me. How can I help?"

She got busy picking her thumbnail. "It's silly. Especially with what you have going on."

"Let me be the judge of that."

She stepped down from the paddock rail, stared somewhere in the region of his neck and mumbled.

Wow, this was hard for her. Normally, he would tease her, but something told him this was not the time. "I didn't quite catch that, Sadie."

"I, um…" A bright pink flush crept up from beneath the collar of her jacket. "I need a plus-one for Blair Bronson's wedding next month, and I wondered if you'd go with me."

Was that all? "Sure."

The tortured look on her face didn't fade, though. "I mean, as a date. Not a *date* date, because we're friends."

Exactly, so she must really want him there if she was asking. "I'm in, Sadie. But what's got you so stressed out?"

"Calling it a date, for one thing." She toed her shoe into the ground. "But there's a reason. This all started because Easton is in the wedding party."

That gaslighting jerk? "I won't let him come within three feet of you, Sadie."

"I'm not worried he'll do something upsetting." Sadie's brief touch on his arm drew his attention. He hadn't realized he'd curled his hands into fists. "We probably won't even talk. Fine by me. I don't want him back."

"I know." Mick would hate it if she did. Easton wasn't

worth the salt in Sadie's tears. "But I can see why you'd want a buddy around, in case it's weird."

"Which is why Blair thought it would be less awkward for me if I had a date. Then Beatie and Dutch overheard."

The situation was crystal clear now. "Let me guess. Dutch and Beatie immediately started playing matchmaker to find you a date?" He'd been targeted by them, too, and for a few years, they'd wanted him and Sadie to go out. He thought they'd finally gotten the message that it was not going to happen.

"They wouldn't listen to a thing I said, so I blurted out that I had it covered, meaning I don't need a date, but they misunderstood and now they expect me to show up with someone." She was talking a mile a minute. "And Beatie was so happy I didn't have the heart to tell her that wasn't what I meant. I decided it would be easier to find a date than explain things and disappoint her."

He pressed his fingers into his palms to keep himself from laughing. "I'm sorry, Sadie. It's not funny but—"

"It is a little funny." Her lips twitched. "If it weren't happening to me, I'd be laughing too. But thanks for playing along as my date."

"We always have a good time, don't we?" It wasn't like they hadn't attended dozens of parties and things together before. And it wasn't like she would get hurt by expecting something to come of it. "What did they say when you told them I'd be your date?"

"I didn't, because I hadn't asked you yet. I told her it'll be a surprise."

"Well, we'll surprise them, for sure. And then they'll realize you can take care of yourself."

"They're motivated by love, but it's so awkward." She shuddered. "Does this make us even now? A BLT and a

Christmas pageant in exchange for scooping pumpkins and one date?"

"It sounds lopsided in my favor. The date is one night. The nativity requires a lot of planning hours between now and December twentieth. Speaking of which, want to grab a pizza? We can brainstorm people who might be willing to serve on the committee, and we can watch some videos Wade sent me for inspiration."

"Sounds like a date." The corner of her mouth twitched. "That was a joke, by the way."

He groaned. "Yeah, yeah."

Because he cared too much about her to ever subject her to a real date with an emotionally unavailable, broken man like himself.

Chapter Three

Midafternoon on Thanksgiving Day, Dove glanced up from mashing potatoes at the island in Natalie's kitchen and smiled as Sadie tucked one last peach rose into the wide brass urn. "That looks fantastic, Sadie."

"Thanks. Not too bad, considering the flowers are all remnants." Left over from her autumn-hued stock, they would soon fade before they sold now that Thanksgiving had arrived, and Sadie hated wasting flowers. She gave a eucalyptus stem a tweak and decided the centerpiece was complete. Not a minute too soon, because the golden-brown turkey had just come out of the oven.

Two cinnamon-tinged pies, apple and pumpkin, cooled on Natalie's kitchen counter, alongside bowls of sage stuffing, vegetables, yeast rolls and Sadie's stove-simmered cranberry sauce. Stomach rumbling, Sadie carried the floral arrangement into the dining room, where she centered it on the table.

Natalie followed her, a steaming casserole dish cradled in her pot holder–clad hands. "Dove's right. The flowers look great, Sadie."

"Thanks. So do those sweet potatoes of Jillian's." She gazed with appreciation at the dish brought by Natalie's mother-in-law, which her elder sister nestled onto a trivet between two place settings at one end of the table.

"Wyatt's Thanksgiving wouldn't be complete without them." Natalie plunged a serving spoon through the marshmallow crust. "Let's see, the table's set. We need to light the candles, but is there anything else missing from the table?"

"The rest of the food," Sadie teased. "And the people." Other than their mom, Yvonne, who was still in the kitchen with Dove, making gravy, the rest of the group watched football in the living room. Even little Rose and Luna McHugh, the orphaned two-and-a-half-year-old twins Natalie and Wyatt had been raising since the death of the girls' parents close to two years ago, joined in the cheering in the other room.

"They can wait a minute. Dove and I want to talk to you."

Dove entered the dining room with the mashed potatoes. "Ooh, did I just overhear that we get to grill her now?"

"Grill me about what?" Sadie had a good idea, though.

"Last Friday, Beatie told us you're taking a mystery date to Blair's wedding." Dove shoved a lock of shoulder-length dark hair behind her ear. "We wanted you to tell us yourself, but you haven't."

"At first, we were curious and excited, but with each passing day, we're wondering *why* you won't tell us. Do you think we won't like him?" Natalie's brow creased.

"That's not it at all. I'm sorry I didn't tell you, but it's been so busy, between work and getting the nativity committee off the ground. And, well, it's a big nothing burger." Sadie glanced at the door to make sure no one was lurking. "Beatie, Dutch and Blair wanted to set me up with a date for the wedding. I said no, I had it covered. I didn't mean I had a date—I meant I didn't need one. But they misunderstood, and it snowballed from there and I didn't know how to get out of it. So I asked Mick to be my plus-one."

"Mick?" Dove yelped. Thankfully, the crowd watching football in the living room let out a cheer.

Sadie waited a moment anyway, in case Mick heard his name and came running. "It's not a real date." Her whisper sounded more like a hiss. "He's doing it in exchange for me helping him with the living nativity."

"No, you'd do it anyway." The perfect curls in Natalie's dark hair swayed as she shook her head. "But maybe he said yes because he has feelings for you."

That was laughable. For one thing, Mick had been dropping hints for years that he intended to remain single.

And for another? "Me, plain as unbuttered bread, with a guy like him? Very funny."

Dove's eyes narrowed. "I don't like when you put yourself down."

"God put a lot of care into creating you, Sadie." Natalie's expression was soft but scolding. "You're pretty, talented and kind."

They were sweet to say such nice things. But Sadie could still hear those fourth-grade girls bullying her. Still remember the boys she'd liked who'd preferred her sisters. Still feel how desperately she'd wanted her parents' attention when they'd focused on her sisters.

Classic middle-child syndrome, as her mom would say if she were to join them in the dining room.

None of those things were her sisters' faults, however. "Thanks, but I assure you, Mick is not interested in me that way. He's doing me a favor, and now I'd like to ask one of you. Will you keep this a secret? We're hoping that Beatie and Dutch will see us together at the wedding, realize we are strictly friends, and give up."

"My lips are sealed. But it's too bad it's not a real date." Natalie adjusted the girls' high chairs.

"I'm bummed." Dove sighed. "I thought this meant you were finally going to have a boyfriend, but I guess you're happy being single."

Sadie bristled like a hedgehog. Singleness was not exactly her choice. She was content with it for now, but—

It wasn't worth having that conversation on Thanksgiving.

While Natalie and Dove slipped out to call the others in for dinner, Sadie stayed behind to tweak the centerpiece once more and take a moment to refocus. Today was about gratitude, not grumbling. She wanted to concentrate on all the blessings God had given her, like the family and friends entering the dining room: Natalie's husband, Wyatt, carrying the roasted turkey on a pewter platter. His parents, Jillian and Gary, each with one of Wyatt and Natalie's twins in arms. Her mom brought out the gravy, and her cousin Thatcher followed, just ahead of Mick.

She caught Mick's eye and smiled but quickly diverted her attention to lighting the candles. Since that disconcerting hug last week, when she'd realized how nice his embrace felt and then been so embarrassed she could have spontaneously combusted, she'd been a little more aware of Mick's proximity than usual. Nothing had changed, exactly, other than a dawning awareness in Sadie that maybe it could.

And that wouldn't do for about a hundred reasons.

The room filled with noise, the snapping of the high chairs' safety-strap buckles over the toddlers' laps and people selecting seats. Wyatt's dad, Mick's uncle Gary, leaned his burly frame against the chair beside Luna's high chair. "Look at this spread."

"Can't wait to dig in." Wyatt fastened a bib with a cartoon

turkey on it around Luna's neck. "But first, let's share what we're thankful for. It's a Dalton family tradition."

And one of Sadie's favorites. She sat beside her dark-haired mom, slipping into one of the two empty seats squeezed at one end of the mahogany expanse. She expected Dove to squish in beside her, but Mick surprised her by dropping into the chair. His lumberjack frame barely fit in the small space.

"Hold hands, everyone," Dove announced.

Sadie caught her mom's soft, cool hand on her right side and, with slight hesitation, Mick's very warm, very large hand on her left. It felt nice, and at the same time weird, because he was her friend, and shouldn't it feel like...nothing?

"I guess I'll go first." Natalie's eyes shone brighter than the candles flickering on the table. "God has blessed us so richly, hasn't He? But I'm especially grateful that the adoption process is almost finished. Just after Christmas, the girls will officially be ours." She beamed at Rose and Luna.

"I second that," Wyatt added, "and I'm also appreciative of your support, Nat, while I strive to be the man, husband and parent God wants me to be. It's been a busy season, with a new business and plans for the therapy ranch in the mix, all while you've worked tirelessly for Foxtail, the girls and me."

The look the newlyweds exchanged was so sweet and tender Sadie had to look away. Would she ever find love like they shared?

It didn't seem likely any time soon.

"Since we're going clockwise, I guess it's my turn." Gary nodded at Wyatt. "I'm happy your new firm is such a success, son."

Mick's hand twitched in Sadie's, an unconscious response that spoke to his tension. The aunt and uncle who'd raised him prioritized the trappings of success, and it sometimes caused friction in the family. Especially since Gary and Jillian didn't understand Mick's or Wyatt's commitment to God. She squeezed his hand ever so slightly.

He squeezed back, so gentle that no one would ever notice, but everyone's attention was on his fashionable aunt Jillian anyway. "I'm thankful for Rose and Luna, the sweetest girls in the world."

The toddlers, adorable in apple-patterned cotton dresses, grinned back. Rose, between Natalie and Wyatt, kicked her legs happily, while Luna, between Wyatt and his dad, shyly tucked in her head.

"I agree. Rose and Luna are worth making the drive to Foxtail Farm, despite all the bad memories of this place." Yvonne, Sadie's mom, had never visited Foxtail before Natalie and Wyatt became guardians of the twins. Everything here reminded her of her ex-husband, Asa. Now she came to see the girls every few months, but she still made her bitterness known. "Asa loved Foxtail more than he loved me, that's for sure."

"Speaking of Foxtail, I'm grateful for our bountiful apple harvest this year." Sadie started talking the moment her mom was finished, hoping to prevent her from complaining more about her deceased dad. At least until later, when they were in private. "I'm also thankful for my family and friends, and that we're all in good health."

"My turn?" Mick shifted, inadvertently drawing Sadie's hand closer to him. "I'm thankful for how we all come together when we need each other."

"You mean all of us helping you with the nativity, right?" Thatcher said, deadpan.

Mick laughed. "Yeah, I guess I do. It wouldn't be happening without you all."

"Not me. I'm not on the committee," Natalie countered.

"But you're praying for us," Mick said, "and that's a vital job."

"My turn." Dove waggled Mick's hand atop the table. "I'm grateful Dutch and Beatie took the week off to visit her sister, because they never take vacation, and if anyone deserves it, they do. And I'm also glad I can FaceTime with Gatlin later."

Poor Dove. It wasn't easy for Sadie's little sister navigating a relationship while Gatlin, a marine, was deployed overseas, but she handled it well.

Then Dove turned to Thatcher beside her. "Now you can go."

"I'm glad my mom is having fun on her Alaskan cruise with her sister, and that I haven't made a mess of Foxtail Ranch yet." Thatcher laughed in his usual self-deprecating manner.

"You're doing great with the ranch." Mick shook his head. "Trust me, the cattle are thriving under your care."

"Thanks, man." With a shake of his head, Thatcher flicked his dark hair from his face without using his hands, a gesture that reminded Sadie of her dad. No surprise there, since her dad and Thatcher's late father had been brothers.

"Let's say grace." Wyatt bowed his head, and Sadie followed suit. After thanking God for His blessings, including the bowls of fragrant food, Mick and her mom released her hands.

Spooning up the sweet potato casserole, Sadie looked at Mick. "Care for some?"

She really shouldn't tease him like this, but that was what she and Mick did. Unlike Wyatt, Mick loathed the casserole. It was the marshmallows. Mick hated them, and no one in his family had ever seemed to notice he disliked the sweets.

Since he couldn't glare at her in the company of both their families, he pressed her leg with his knee beneath the table, a subtle message that he knew what she was doing. "Thanks, Sadie. Here, I'll serve up some broccoli for you."

He forked a spear from the platter in front of him and dropped it onto her plate.

Touché. It was her least favorite vegetable, which he knew.

But neither of them could resist Dove's yeast rolls. When the basket came around, though, Mick set it down. "I'll just eat Luna's. I doubt she wants her roll."

Sadie bit back a laugh because everyone knew how much Luna loved bread. And how much Mick enjoyed teasing the girls.

Sure enough, little Luna giggled and covered the crumbled remains of her roll with her dimpled hands. "Nah, Unka Mick! *My* bwead!"

"*Cousin* Mick," Jillian interjected.

The words weren't harsh, but they were firm. Who knew Jillian was such a stickler for specific family titles?

Luna's brow pinched in confusion, though, so Sadie gestured at Dove, Thatcher and Mick. "In our dad's family, Jillian, adults are often called *uncle* and *aunt*, so that's how we've been referring to ourselves around the girls."

"It's up to Wyatt and Natalie what terms the girls use, of course, but Mick is Wyatt's cousin, and we wouldn't want Rose and Luna confused." Jillian sipped her water.

"I don't care what they call me." Mick spooned cranberry sauce onto his plate. "As long as we're buds—right, girls?"

"My bwead." Luna grinned, while Rose covered her mouth with one dimpled hand, then flung out her arm to blow him a kiss. Everyone laughed, and Sadie's heart melted like the butter atop the mashed potatoes.

After eating a full meal, including a slice of Dove's apple pie, Sadie glanced at her watch. "I hate to excuse myself, but the farmstand won't decorate itself. I'd better step out before the sun goes down."

"We said we'd help." Thatcher pushed back his chair.

"I know, but I don't want to rush anyone."

"I'm finished." Dove patted her lips with her napkin. "Let's go."

Wyatt's parents and Mom stayed behind with Natalie to clean the dishes and bathe the twins while the rest of them donned their jackets and strode across the leaf-strewn path to the farmstand. Thankfully, Thatcher and Wyatt had already retrieved all the labeled boxes and bins of Foxtail's decor and stacked them inside the farmstand. "The outdoor lights are already out front, though," Thatcher confirmed.

"I'll hang those." Mick grabbed one of the two ladders Wyatt had set out earlier.

"The outlet is behind the birdhouse by the door," Sadie instructed. "I guess I'll work on the tractor." Tourists liked to take photos in front of Sadie's seasonal displays and the vintage John Deere tractor permanently parked in front of the farmstand. And when those photos were posted online, they served as free advertising. Which, frankly, Foxtail Farm could use. Their dad hadn't left things in the best shape financially.

Sadie scooped up a lightweight bin labeled *Tractor* and strode out into the brisk twilight. Mick was wedged behind the rustic six-foot birdhouse by the door that hid the outlet panel, with an extension cord trailing behind him like a tail. Then the bundles of white fairy lights came to life.

"Hooray!" Sadie set down the bin. "I'm always relieved when they work."

"If they didn't, I would find new ones for you. I know how important Black Friday is to retail establishments, and shoppers expect holiday decor."

"It's true." But she wasn't thinking about holiday-weekend sales. She was feeling grateful for him. What a good guy he was, helping her family like this. No complaints, no hesitation.

She knew all that already, of course, but tonight, as he climbed the ladder and got to work in the soft glow of the twinkling lights, something shifted inside her.

If she weren't careful, she could be in danger of repeating her adolescent crush on Mick.

But this time, there could be consequences. Bad ones.

Hanging the light strings on the under-eave hooks was quick work, and it wasn't long before Mick came to the end of the farmstand's facade. From his spot on the ladder they looked all right, even and taut. One problem, though. Three coils of light strings remained on the ground, ready for use.

"Hey, Sadie?"

"Yeah?" She looked up from draping a pine swag over the vintage tractor's bright green canopy.

"Did I do something wrong? Because there are a lot of lights left over."

"Oh, sorry. Those aren't for the eaves, they're for the farmhouse." The old home that had belonged to her great-grandparents had been divided into tiny apartments where she, Thatcher and Dove lived, mere yards from the farmstand. "Do you mind helping me hang these from the overhangs?" She gestured to a pile of rustic lanterns and jingle bells the size of soccer balls, all topped with faux pine and red bows.

He scaled down the ladder. "No problem."

When that was finished, they placed two six-foot nutcrackers at the entrance to the farmstand.

"That's the last of it." Sadie adjusted one of the nutcrackers an inch to the left. "For tonight, anyway. I can't make up my displays until the Christmas trees arrive tomorrow. Thanks for your help."

"My pleasure. It felt good to get outside and burn off some pumpkin pie calories too. Everything tasted amazing. Except for the sweet potatoes."

She snickered. "Do you forgive me for making you eat them?"

"I'll forgive you for anything, even that casserole. But you deserved the broccoli."

"It was worth it to see the look on your face. But I hope you noticed that I tried not to give you too many marshmallows when I spooned the serving on your plate."

"Thanks for that small mercy. Who invented marshmallows, anyway?"

"A culinary genius."

"That's not what I was going to say. At all." He stepped back to take in the decorations. "How does it look?"

"Beautiful, but let's walk over there so we can get a fuller view. Back to the important matter of who invented marshmallows," she said as they walked into the parking lot. "I think it was the ancient Egyptians."

"I can believe that. I've eaten marshmallows so stale they could easily have been three thousand years old."

Her laugh was sweet. "Well, I watched your aunt open a fresh package for tonight's casserole. She measured out an exact cup of mini marshmallows for the topping—I'm not that precise when I cook. But I guess she's a stickler about things like recipes. And using precise terms for family members, wanting the girls to call you *cousin* instead of *uncle*."

Mick had hoped no one would think twice about that part of their dinner conversation, but Sadie was too observant. He shrugged, as if it hadn't bothered him. "It's up to Wyatt and Natalie what the girls call me. I don't care, as long as they don't call me…late for dinner."

Sadie groaned. "That joke is about as old as those Egyptian marshmallows. But I'm serious. It was a big enough deal for Jillian to voice it at the table. Do you think she's that way because of your mom?"

Sadie knew all about Mick's parents. How his dad had left before Mick could walk, how his mom had struggled with alcohol addiction and left him with Jillian and Gary when he was five so she could go to rehab. How she had reclaimed him but brought him back within a week, starting an irregular cycle that repeated a few times during his childhood.

The last time he saw his mom, he was in high school. She had been clear-eyed, charming and insistent that she'd be back for his graduation. But instead, she had driven while intoxicated the next week and had died in a single-car collision.

It was painful, yes, but it had nothing to do with Aunt Jillian correcting Rose and Luna at the table. "How so?"

"Maybe Jillian is sensitive about terminology because she and your mom were sisters and she didn't want you to get confused. Your identity as Rose and Luna's cousin—once they're legally adopted, that's what you'll officially be to them—helps them grow up knowing their place in a family they weren't born into."

"They're young enough, I'm not sure it matters."

"I guess you're right. She's just a stickler." Sadie chuckled.

But Mick didn't join her. Aunt Jillian wasn't a stickler because she loved rules. And her comment hadn't been about the girls knowing their place.

It was about Mick knowing his.

Because while Gary and Jillian had raised him alongside Wyatt, it had always been clear that Mick was not their son.

When he was eight or nine, he'd overheard his aunt tell Wyatt that Mick wasn't a member of the family the way Wyatt was. He'd taken it to mean that he wasn't their son the way Wyatt was, but after a while, he'd realized that while they were vocal about their love for Wyatt, they'd never told Mick they loved him.

Not once.

Neither had Grandpa Hank. That said, all three adults in Mick's life had nurtured him, supported him and encouraged his love of animals. And after Grandpa Hank had secured a promise from Mick that he would stay in Goldenrod and work at his veterinary clinic, he'd left him his share of the partnership with Leonard Coggins before passing away a few years ago.

His family knew him well. And they cared for him. But they didn't love him.

Mick saw evidence time and again, on occasions like tonight when Jillian made sure he knew he wasn't really their son and therefore not Rose and Luna's uncle. Or when Wyatt left town to follow his job a few years ago without explanation or keeping in touch.

It turned out Wyatt had had secret reasons, but it still hurt that he hadn't trusted Mick enough to confide in him. To let Mick be there for him.

Mick had craved words of love when he was younger. As a teenager, he'd determined he would someday have his own family. To that end, he'd invested his whole heart in a girl who'd ultimately rejected him. He'd tried again with another young woman in veterinary school, but the results were the same, and it was then that he'd realized what the problem was.

Him.

There was something wrong with him, where anyone who should have loved him left, and the ones who stuck around held him at arm's length.

Only animals had offered unconditional love until he'd met God several years ago. For the first time, he'd felt like he had met Someone who would never abandon him.

But he was too flawed or broken for human love, so he'd decided singleness was the best way to protect himself from further hurt. He devoted himself to animals, and let things lie with his aunt and uncle because they avoided unpleasant conversations at all costs. Besides, they couldn't help it if they didn't love him, could they?

He'd come to terms with it and realized there was something to be said for knowing where he stood with people.

Still, the old wound ached in his gut as he stared up at the stars coming out, and he was grateful he and Sadie weren't standing face-to-face, because she didn't miss things. Even though it was dark, she would see his pain.

So he did what he always did. Changed the subject. "It looks great, Sadie."

"Thanks to you. I love the view, but my feet are starting to freeze." She stamped them on the ground. "Let's go help them finish up inside, and then I think some hot cocoa is in order."

He was thankful for Sadie. Thankful they had a strong friendship that had stood the test of time, and he was confident it always would. He was grateful nothing would ever change between them, because life without her was unthinkable.

"I'm in." He joined her walking back. "As long as the hot cocoa doesn't have any marshmallows in it."

Something had to change.

As the clock ticked toward midnight, Sadie curled up on

the love seat in her quadrant of the old farmhouse, a mug of chamomile tea warming her hands and an open Bible on the table beside her.

Help me wait on You, Lord. To be patient.

But now that the busyness of Thanksgiving Day was over, she felt empty. Not just lonely, but yearning.

The need for change gnawed at Sadie like an itch.

What had Dove said before dinner? *I guess you're happy being single.* She hadn't meant any harm by it, but her words stung.

Sadie was grateful for her life, but she wanted true love and a family of her own. And it was becoming clearer with every passing season that it wouldn't—couldn't—happen in Goldenrod. No amount of matchmaking by Beatie, Dutch or Blair would change that.

She'd had one relationship. Before and since Easton Morris, no one had expressed interest in her. Sitting at the Thanksgiving table, witnessing loving couples and children, made her keenly aware that time was passing her by.

But she wasn't just dissatisfied personally. Professionally too. Two years from now, when her mandatory time at Foxtail Farm was up, she did not want to be caught flat-footed, with a thin résumé and outdated skills. She must start working on improving herself now so she would be ready: It was time to learn, grow and network. And maybe within these next two years she could save enough to start her own shop in a larger town, away from the competition of Goldenrod Floral Design.

And where she might have a better opportunity to meet Mr. Right.

The thought of leaving Goldenrod caused physical pain in her chest. She loved her family and friends. But her sisters and Thatcher had their own lives. Mick had his.

Her eyes drifted shut. The summer she'd first met Mick, when she was a middle schooler full of fancy, she'd decided he was the One. She'd felt it so strongly that she'd written it in her diary.

I feel so light I could probably fly away.

Teenage fluff. As she'd matured her crush had faded, and she and Mick had remained friends even though they hadn't always lived in the same town. She'd spent the school year in San Diego with her mom, and he'd left for vet school. But they'd always stayed in touch and found their easy rapport every time they reunited.

After his heart was broken twice by the most foolish women in the universe, as far as Sadie was concerned, he'd made it clear that he never intended to marry.

Right then, she'd realized if she wanted Mick in her life, it would have to be as friends. She'd stood by that choice.

But she couldn't ignore her desire for love, marriage, children. A satisfying career. Things she didn't have here in Goldenrod.

After a quick prayer and a deep breath, she pulled her laptop off the coffee table. The sleeping machine came to life with a soft whir and glow of light.

She tapped into her emails, scrolled back to find the one from Ruth about the internship and clicked the embedded link. She probably wouldn't be accepted, so she wouldn't tell her family yet, but she needed to try.

She typed her name in the application.

Chapter Four

Sadie glanced at her watch the following Saturday afternoon and groaned. Blair's wedding was in a few hours, and she was still covered in pine needles.

So many pine needles she looked like she'd wrestled a Christmas tree. But as she knelt in the church aisle to secure the last of the pew decorations, she realized several frosted eucalyptus leaves had also attached themselves to her cream fleece jacket, along with stray petals, bits of ribbon threads and blobs of sap.

Nothing unusual for her, but poor Mick was more accustomed to being covered in pet hair than pine and peonies. He was such a good sport, helping her decorate the church sanctuary for Blair's wedding later today.

And for being her date.

Which was, of course, no big deal, even though thinking about it caused a shiver to traverse her spine.

She snuck glances at him as he placed a large floral arrangement on a pedestal beside the altar. His eyes narrowed as he studied the flowers, rotated them a few degrees to the left, then nodded in satisfaction.

"Looks perfect." It felt a little odd to raise her voice inside church, but she wasn't sure he could hear her otherwise.

"I was going to say the same about your other arrangements. It smells good in here too. Like Christmas and Valentine's Day all at once."

An apt description for a December wedding.

"I'm so grateful for your help, but I didn't intend to put you to work today, Mick. Honest."

"I offered."

"True, but you've already done so much for me lately. Scooping pumpkins, decorating the farmstand, this—plus being my date today." She rose from the floor and fluffed out the ribbon she'd just tied around the pew. "It's been so busy since Thanksgiving I haven't been able to get you that BLT I owe you."

Thanksgiving weekend was always busy, with long days at the farmstand and evenings spent with her mom, whose visits were few and far between. This year, once Mom left town, Sadie had missed a day of work due to a migraine— triggered by fatigue, probably. Despite her absence, the nativity committee had finalized the route for the walkthrough event, and the actors had all been selected.

Good thing, because the nativity was only two weeks away.

"We'll get that BLT sooner or later." Mick folded his arms across his gray down vest, straining the blue flannel of his shirtsleeves over his impressive biceps. "But I'm the one who owes you. I would be toast by now if you didn't have the living nativity responsibilities all mapped out. You think of things that hadn't occurred to me at all, like additional lighting and signage. All I've done for you today is carry things in from the minivan, nothing big. You're the one who crafted these masterpieces."

His compliment warmed her insides. "Thanks, but I would say being my date today is a big deal."

His eyebrow quirked. "Because Easton Morris will be here?"

"No. I mean, it's not like I think about him at all anymore, but betrayals leave scars, you know?"

"Do I ever." Mick must be thinking of the women he had dated who had broken his heart, but he offered Sadie an encouraging smile. "Hopefully, you don't have to talk to him, but if you do, I'll be right beside you."

"To be honest, it's his fiancée who bothers me more. Not just because of how she and Easton were sneaking behind my back, but since I met her in ballet class the first summer I spent at Foxtail Farm with my dad—"

"She's Ballet Girl?" His eyes went wide. "The one who called you names?"

"You remember that? Yeah." They'd just been kids, and Sadie had forgiven, even if she hadn't quite forgotten. *Lord, help me be free of the pain of those memories. To more fully love and forgive the people who hurt me.* Even if their words still poked her wounds.

Enough of that. "There's less than two hours until Blair walks down the aisle. Good thing we're pretty much finished here. I need to vacuum up my mess and take the boutonnieres to the library, where the groomsmen will gather before the ceremony."

"I'll take care of those now." Mick scooped up the small box on a pew full of sprays she had crafted for the male members of the wedding party. "I assume this is the groom's boutonniere on the end because it's different. I don't recognize this flower."

"Christmas rose." As she explained the legend to him, she unwound the cord on her portable vacuum. "They're native to Europe, not Israel, but it's still a lovely reminder that God provides."

"And He wants us to use our talents for Him. Like in 'The Little Drummer Boy.' An oldie but a goodie for a reason." Mick headed out of the sanctuary. "Be back in a sec."

"Thanks." Sadie retreated to the entrance of the sanctuary, where she'd seen an outlet. It also afforded her a good view of the entire space. The large floral arrangements flanking the dark-wood altar appeared evenly spaced, as did the candelabras she had embellished with miniature versions of the bridesmaids' bouquets. Larger bouquets in winter-white urns stood on pedestals at the doors and altar rail. The pew decorations were level. As the church's central-heating system came on, a few ribbons fluttered in the current of forced air emanating from the floor vents, but the compositions all stayed secure in their places. Phew.

As she finished vacuuming, Mick reappeared. "All set. Anything else to do here?"

She shook her head. "I delivered the centerpieces to the reception venue this morning, and the bridal party shouldn't need any help." Boutonnieres and corsages weren't difficult to pin, and the flower crown she had crafted for the junior bridesmaid was a snap to put on. "There's time to grab a coffee from the shop next door before we have to change clothes for the ceremony. It's no BLT, but it's my treat." They had each brought garment bags with them so they could switch from their jeans into more suitable wedding attire once they finished setting up the flowers.

"Actually, I just realized I left my dress shoes at home. I can't exactly wear these to the wedding." He grimaced at his scuffed, stained work boots. "Is it all right if I borrow your minivan to run home?"

"Sure, if you don't mind putting my vacuum in the back of the van." She dug her keys out of the front pocket of her dark-rinse jeans. "But you don't need to change your shoes on my account."

"This is a date, Sadie, so I want to look my best." His smile was part playful, part endearing. He was such a good friend.

"Thanks, Mick."

He gathered the vacuum and his garment bag from the pew in the back row. After sending her a wave, he disappeared from the church.

She picked up her own garment bag and made her way to the office wing of the church, where she shouldn't encounter any of the bridal party or guests. She intended to leave her garment bag in the ladies' room while she hopped out for a peppermint latte, but then she caught her reflection beneath the bathroom's fluorescent lights.

Her hair draped in shades of drying straw, brown to gold. Faint freckles spattered over a not-quite-straight nose, and darker eyes than her sisters had. Never the sort to be high maintenance about her hair and makeup, she'd gone simple this morning with a bun at her nape and a light application of blush. She had packed her makeup bag and curling iron, however, in case she needed a quick touch-up once she changed.

Mick was being so sweet about ensuring he had the right shoes, making an effort for their fake date. Maybe she ought to look special too.

Forget the peppermint latte. She plugged in the curling iron.

Halfway through her hair, her phone pinged and a message appeared on her screen.

I am so sorry but Fly rolled in something nasty. Do U mind if I take care of it? Hate to leave U stranded tho.

Mind? Hardly. This was perfect. Not for Mick, having

to give his sweet but stinky dog a bath. But for her to finish putting on her face, as Beatie would phrase it.

Glad you didn't change into your good clothes yet! Take your time. Meet you at twenty 'til the hour in the courtyard?

He sent back a thumbs-up emoji.

Half an hour later, hair curled, mascara applied and wearing a sage green dress, she stepped out of the ladies' room. Voices raised in conversation grew louder with every step she took toward the sanctuary, telling her the wedding party had arrived. Maybe even a few guests too.

She entered the narthex, curious what she'd find. And then her curiosity died.

It was *him*. Easton Morris, dressed in a tailored charcoal suit. Staring right at her.

Well, Mick might not be here to bolster her, but that didn't mean she was alone. Jesus had promised never to forsake her, hadn't He?

Lord, help me to not do or say anything that would dishonor You.

"Hello." She smiled at him but didn't slow her pace.

"Wait up, Sadie. I need to ask you something."

Great. Sadie spun on her low gold-toned heels, clutching her wrap and purse against her stomach.

Easton, dark hair flopping in charming disarray over his brow, grinned like he didn't have any qualms about being around her after what he did. "You did all the flowers, didn't you?"

Why was he asking that? *Please don't ask me to do the flowers for your wedding. Please just say they look nice.*

She took a deep breath. "Yes, I did."

"Well, I stabbed myself twice trying to put this thing on by myself. I don't know if mine is extra thick or something, because it's a beast. Can you do it for me?" He held out one of the boutonnieres.

She was willing to admit boutonnieres could be tricky, but his was not deliberately *extra thick*. And the thought of taking it from his hand and pinning it on the lapel of his rented suit made her stomach flop. Not because she was afraid she'd catch one whiff of his cologne and feel heartbroken all over again, but because it felt like too intimate a gesture considering she had expected to be his fiancée, right up until the moment he dumped her. Even for two tearful weeks after that, she'd clung to the hope of a reconciliation, until Mick saw him with Hallie.

His now-fiancée. If anyone pinned a boutonniere on Easton, it should be her.

Sadie stared him in the eye. "I'm sure Hallie's around somewhere. She can help you."

"She's outside."

"That's where I'm headed too. I can send her in if you like."

"I can't wait that long. I'm a groomsman and I'm supposed to be ushering when guests arrive. There are a few people already here. Come on, Sadie, please?"

Sure enough, an older woman in a purple satin suit entered the sanctuary. Spying them, she offered a self-deprecating chuckle. "I'm a friend of the bride's grandmother. Which side am I supposed to sit on? I don't know if things like that matter anymore, but I'm old-school."

"I'd be honored to help with that in just a moment, ma'am. Once I look the part of a proper groomsman." Easton's lopsided smile made the woman giggle.

Sadie was not impressed by his Prince Charming act, but he was right. He had a job to do, and the flower on his lapel was arguably part of the uniform. If she refused to help him, she would look petty.

"Fine." She shoved her clutch purse and wrap beneath one arm, snatched the pine and rose spray from his palm, and hoped he knew she could stab him with the straight pin if she really wanted to.

Mick didn't recognize the woman in the narthex as Sadie. Not at first.

She and the male figure formed a pair of silhouettes until his eyes adjusted to the dimmer light after being out in the sun-bright courtyard. Then, slowly, he could distinguish their faces. Sadie, fussing with that creep Easton's boutonniere?

An unpleasant sensation washed over him. The last time he'd felt like this was when he was seven or eight, wishing on his birthday candles that he could trade places with his cousin Wyatt and be secure in a family, jealous—

Mick almost choked. No way was he jealous of Easton Morris.

Angry, sure. The guy hadn't treated Sadie honorably. Maybe what he felt most was disgust with himself, because he hadn't been there to protect Sadie as he had promised.

He was at her side in three long strides. "Sadie, there you are."

She hopped back from Easton as if she hadn't wanted Mick to see what she was doing. "I hope you haven't been outside waiting long."

"Not at all." Mick's chin lifted. "Easton."

"Mick." Easton's smile didn't falter, but his eyes hardened. "Long time no see."

That was the way Mick liked it, frankly. His hand slipped

around Sadie's waist. Hopefully, she'd understand that he was here for her.

A woman in purple old enough to be their grandma rapped Easton playfully on the arm. "Are you ready for me now?"

"I am indeed." Easton offered her his arm and escorted the woman into the sanctuary.

Mick's hand shifted to rest at the small of Sadie's back. "Shall we get some air?"

"Yes, please." It came out muddled, like one word.

He guided her outside, down the church steps. "Are you okay? Dumb question. I'm sorry I wasn't there when you needed me."

At a brick planter of evergreen jasmine, she turned to face him. Smiling. "Honestly, I'm glad I was by myself. God answered my prayers, because I handled it in a way where I have no regrets. I feel fine, relieved I'm not married to a guy like that."

"That's wonderful. And I'm glad you didn't marry him, too." Because the thought of her with someone who didn't appreciate her added fuel to the fire burning in his gut. "You're one brave woman."

"I don't know about that, but thanks for being here for me. And dressing up so handsomely, in your good shoes and everything."

Mick could've kicked himself for not complimenting her right off the bat, but since seeing her with Easton, he'd been so focused on how she was doing internally that he hadn't cast a single thought for her outward appearance. Not that he ever really paid attention to what she wore.

But now he looked at her—really looked at her—and... was his tie too tight? Because all of a sudden, it was hard to swallow. That dress was...

Wow, okay. Modest, but cut just right to accentuate her pretty figure. It had to be new, because if she'd worn that stunning gray-green dress before, he'd have remembered.

And it wasn't just the dress that caught his attention, or how she had styled her hair into soft curls that highlighted the gentle curve of her rosy cheeks. There was a sparkle in her eyes that spoke of confidence. Kindness. Excitement.

Everything about her was...

"Beautiful."

Great. He finally remembered how to swallow, but in the process, he forgot how to speak in complete sentences.

Normally, he wouldn't allow himself to think about Sadie like this. They were friends, and while she was pretty, he had no business looking at her that way. But today, he couldn't help it.

"You like my dress?" She gave a little turn, and the hem of her dress twirled around her knees. "It's been in the back of my closet forever. I finally had the chance to wear it." Then she looked over his shoulder. "Guess who's crossing the street?"

Mick turned to see Dutch and Beatie enter the courtyard's wrought iron gate arm in arm. "I guess it's time for the big mystery-date reveal."

"Sadie?" A desperate voice drew them around. A middle-aged woman with a corsage pinned to her dark green suit hurried down the church steps. "We need you."

"Of course!" Sadie took the woman's outstretched hand but turned back to Mick before mounting the steps. "Go ahead and take a seat. I'll find you."

As she disappeared into the church, a thud and a soft cry behind him turned him back around. Beatie was on the ground beside one of the brick planters, and Dutch was bent over, assisting her.

Mick was at her side in less than a second. "Beatie, are you okay?"

"I'm fine, just embarrassed." Beatie pushed herself up to sit. "I wasn't paying attention, and I walked right into the brick."

He shifted to support her back. "Did you hit your head? Want to see a doctor?"

"No and no." Beatie's tone was harsher than usual. "I just want up on my feet."

"Sure thing." He and Dutch helped her back on her feet.

Dutch wrapped his arm around his wife. "Maybe we should go home, so you can put your feet up."

"Stop fussing. I'm fine—or I will be, once I brush the dust off." Beatie used the back of her hand to swat a streak of dirt on her maroon pants. "Before my little spill, Mick, I saw Sadie run up into the church. Didn't get a good look at her, but I imagine she was spiffed up for her date."

"Yep, she looked nice." Mick tugged at the collar of his blue dress shirt.

Dutch tucked Beatie's hand into the crook of his arm, pulling her close. "Who was she with, Mick?"

"The bride's mom, I think."

"No, I mean her date. Do you know who he is?"

Before Mick could say *You're looking at him*, Beatie tugged Dutch by the sleeve of his camel sports coat. "Let's just go see for ourselves. Besides, I'd like to go in from the cold."

Judging by the way Beatie hobbled toward the sanctuary, it wasn't the temperature bothering her as much as her hip. Mick winced, imagining the bruise she would be sporting later.

But at least, for the moment, he didn't have to confess he was Sadie's so-called date.

Back inside, he couldn't see Sadie in the narthex with the other guests, but since she'd been summoned by Blair's mom, she was probably occupied in the bridal dressing room. He would wait a few minutes, even though Sadie said to be seated without her.

Then the crowd thickened. He took a wedding program and then paced the narthex, reading the placards beneath the stained-glass windows streaming a rainbow's worth of color against the eggshell walls. The minutes ticked by.

Maybe he should take a seat after all.

There was no room in Dutch and Beatie's pew toward the front, so he slipped into a spot near the back, setting Sadie's program on the red cushion beside him to save her a spot. His gaze shifted as Easton walked up the side aisle, escorting a woman whose tuxedo cat was a patient at the clinic, and it made Mick's blood heat up again.

Watching Easton and his smug smile saunter back down the aisle, Mick made a decision.

Sadie deserved a lot better than having that guy as her only experience with dating. She was kind, funny, smart, talented and pretty.

No, beautiful.

And today, he intended to give Sadie the best date—real *or* fake—of her life.

Chapter Five

Sadie knocked for what felt like the twentieth time on the bathroom stall door. "Kelsey? Won't you come out so I can fix it?"

When Sadie had followed Blair's mom into the room reserved for the bridesmaids, she had been grateful for the zipper pouch in her purse full of floral tape, safety pins, Band-Aids and scissors. But none of those items were required, or useful, when the crying middle schooler had run, in a blur of scarlet chiffon, into the bathroom, where she'd locked herself in a stall.

Sadie knew Kelsey from church. Not well, but they'd served hot chocolate together at last year's Sunday school Christmas party. Blair's young cousin was a sweetheart, but something was truly upsetting her, and according to Blair's mom, it had to do with the flower crown.

Sadie knocked gently on the stall door. "Is it too small? Does it pinch? Because I can adjust it so it's more comfortable."

Kelsey's sniff echoed in the tile chamber. "That's not it."

Okay, it wasn't the size. Was it the appearance? "If the flowers flopped, I can fix that too. I have all kinds of tricks for last-minute problems. Pins, clips, even glue dots in my bag."

"It's not the flowers. It's my…" Her voice trailed off.

Her what? If not the flowers, was it her hair?

Blair's mom pointed at her watch. Oh dear, it was now two minutes until the official wedding time. "If you can't get her out in five minutes," Mrs. Bronson whispered, "we'll have to start without her."

Sadie nodded as the bride's mom left the bathroom. She prayed silently for help.

Her eye caught on her garment bag, which she had left hanging over the back of the chair in the corner. "Your aunt is gone now, Kelsey. I'm going to plug in my curling iron for a quick touch-up. You're welcome to use it too."

Thankfully, it was a quick-heat model. Sadie grabbed a random chunk of her hair and clamped it in the iron.

The stall door unlocked with a soft click, but Sadie made sure her gaze fixed on her own reflection, not on Kelsey. The last thing she wanted to do was make the girl feel self-conscious. She continued curling her already-curled hair while Kelsey retrieved a brown paper towel from the automatic dispenser and ran it beneath the faucet.

"It's my hair," she murmured. "Blair said my curls covered the flowers in the back."

Sadie set the curling iron on the edge of a sink. "I'm sure she didn't mean it in a bad way, but let me check." Shifting behind Kelsey, she saw the problem at once. "There's one flower right in the back that's too small for your gorgeous big curls. My fault, because I should have taken your hair into account when I designed the crown. I'm no hairdresser, but if it's all right with you, I could use the curling iron to tweak this tiny section of hair around that pesky flower and pin it in place."

"Okay." Kelsey swiped her cheeks with the damp paper towel.

Sadie got to work. "You have stunning hair. I'm so envious."

"It's not stunning." Kelsey stared down at the sink. "I'm so ugly."

"Kelsey, no. Is this about more than your hair? You don't like the dress? Wearing the flowers?"

"I don't like *me*." Kelsey sniffed.

"Honey." Sadie unplugged the curling iron and enveloped the girl in a gentle hug.

Middle school was the worst. Growth spurts, hormones out of whack and not feeling comfortable in your own skin. Add an offhand comment by the bride, and Kelsey must have been overcome with uncomfortable emotions.

Sadie was long out of middle school, but she could still relate. "It's easy to compare ourselves to others and judge our appearances harshly, especially when we're subjected to ridiculous standards on social media. But you are not ugly."

"My braces look bad." Kelsey pulled out of the hug but remained close enough for Sadie to pat her back. "And I'm not as pretty as Blair and her friends. I'll look awful in photos with them."

"Braces can feel awkward, sure, but they're short-term. And I disagree with the rest of what you said. When Blair looks at those photos in future years, it will be with joy that you, her favorite cousin, were in her wedding. But more than that. You know the Bible says we are fearfully and wonderfully made, right? When God created you, He gave you so many beautiful attributes. A warm smile that makes me happy whenever I see it. A gentle spirit and kind heart. Love for others and for Him. That's lasting beauty. But, for the record, you are pretty too."

"You really think so?"

"Oh yes. It's hard, but try not to compare yourself to anyone else. Be Kelsey, a person God wanted in the world, who happens to be beautiful inside and out."

Kelsey looked at herself in the mirror. Took a deep breath. "Is it too late to be in the wedding?"

Sadie glanced at her watch. "Not if we leave right now."

When Kelsey nodded, Sadie guided her out of the bathroom and down the hall. They rushed to the narthex, where Blair, resplendent in an elegant gown of white lace, stood with her hand crooked into her dad's arm. The bridesmaids formed a line ahead of her, ready to enter the sanctuary.

Blair broke into a wide grin. "I'm glad you made it, Kelsey."

"We brought your bouquet, Kelsey." One of the bridesmaids scooped it off the guest book table.

Sadie sent a grateful prayer to God that no one had scolded Kelsey but instead welcomed her with smiles. Kelsey gave Sadie a brief wave before finding her place in line, and at that moment, they began the procession inside the church.

Once Blair and her dad were down the aisle, Sadie ducked into the sanctuary. Phew. Mick had chosen a seat in the back, so she could sneak in easier. She slid in beside him while the pastor offered his opening remarks.

Mick shifted to make room for her. "Is everything okay?"

She nodded, and they turned their attention to the wedding. It was sweet and lovely, but Sadie's thoughts kept returning to her minutes with Kelsey. How well Sadie understood feeling like the plainest person in a group. Yet she had reminded Kelsey that God viewed her as precious. Beautiful.

Words she never spoke to herself.

She'd told herself the opposite, in fact, all those times she avoided looking in the mirror because she didn't want to see her imperfections. Or those moments she felt overlooked or straight-up disparaged. It wasn't about vanity or pride.

It was about esteem. Feeling valued.

Why, why would she remind herself of the negative names that childhood bullies had called her but not of the far nicer things God called her?

She had offered advice to Kelsey she hadn't taken herself.

Lord, I have been listening to the wrong voices. Help me hear Your voice and view myself as You do, and to find my worth in You alone.

God had given her so many gifts, including the friendship of the man sitting beside her.

Mick must have felt her gaze, because he glanced at her. Then he offered his hand. She rested hers in his, and he squeezed it.

It wasn't a real date. She knew that. But holding his hand felt nice.

Just like that hug had, before Thanksgiving.

She wouldn't overthink it. She would just live in the moment and enjoy the warmth of Mick's hand for another minute.

Mick held Sadie's hand until the happy couple were pronounced husband and wife, and then they joined the rest of the congregation in applause.

Once the wedding party exited the sanctuary and the other guests began moving, Sadie gathered her purse from the floor. "Wasn't that lovely?"

"It was." He may not know either the bride or groom well, but the ceremony had been focused on the foundation of Jesus, which he appreciated.

"Ooh, here come the Underhills. What did they say when you told them you're my mystery date?"

"I didn't get a chance to." Not after Beatie had tumbled. "What do you think they'll say?"

"Let's find out." Sadie smiled at their approaching

friends. Dutch rubbed his hands together and Beatie smiled tentatively, as if she weren't sure what to make of what she was seeing. As soon as they were close enough for conversation, Sadie made jazz hands. "Ta-da!"

"Is this a real date?" Beatie's hands went to her hips.

"Nah, they pulled a fast one on us." Dutch shook his head. "This is a friend thing."

"Why can't it be both?" Mick wrapped an arm around Sadie's shoulders.

She leaned into him, smelling of flowers. "A real date, among friends."

Beatie scowled. "It's not a date if it's friends."

"We had this coming, I suppose." Dutch didn't seem as disgruntled as Beatie. "Now, wife of mine, what do you say we head to the reception before all the good parking spaces are taken?"

A good idea, considering Beatie might not feel up to walking far after falling in the courtyard. "We'll see you at the party. I think we need to clean up flowers first. Right, Sadie?"

"No, actually, but—you two go on. See you shortly." Sadie kissed both Beatie's and Dutch's cheeks, then turned back to Mick. "My work for the day is done. The arrangements belong to Blair, to keep, donate or toss as she chooses."

"Toss?" All these beautiful arrangements, after hours and hours of Sadie's work? "That seems like a huge waste."

"But that's what happens after a lot of weddings and funerals, for various reasons. People have allergies, transportation issues or lack space at home." Her mouth twisted. "I suggested to Blair that she speak to the church in advance about leaving the larger arrangements here, to be enjoyed at worship service tomorrow. But I doubt they'll keep the pew decorations."

"Will they go in the trash?"

"I hope not. I mentioned to Blair that if no one can use them, I'd be happy to take them back home with me. I could break them into smaller arrangements to donate to the nursing home. I do that with things that don't sell at the farmstand, pick out the flowers that haven't faded and give them away so less goes to waste. I'm always short of vases for things like that, though, so I've been saving jars." She scanned the room, looking wistfully at her creations. "But anyway, Blair never got back to me, so we don't need to move the flowers back to Foxtail. Give me a minute to grab my garment bag from the restroom, and then we can go."

When she returned, he took the bag from her and pushed open the sanctuary door. A brisk gust of wind hit them full in the face.

"Weather's changing," he said.

"It definitely feels like winter." Sadie rubbed her arms. "Where did you park the minivan?"

"I hope you don't mind, but I stopped by Foxtail to trade it for my truck. It's just down the street, but in the meantime, wear this." He laid her garment bag over the stair rail, shrugged out of his sports coat and wrapped it around her shoulders. "If you like, we can run back to your house to pick up a heavier coat, or you can just wear this."

"I'll be okay, if you don't mind me borrowing this. I'll give it back to you at the reception. It should be toasty warm at the hotel ballroom." She snuggled deeper into his coat.

"I won't want it. You know that I always run hot." But once they were inside the truck, he set the heat to max for her.

They chatted and teased each other about the differences in their temperature preferences over the short drive to the hotel, and within minutes, they were inside the ballroom. Signs of Sadie's hard work graced every table, from the pine sprigs attached to snowflake photo-frame ornaments that served as place cards to the pretty centerpieces. They found their as-yet-unoccupied table across the room from Beatie and Dutch's. "Here we are. Sadie Dalton and 'Sadie Dalton's guest.'" Mick held back a laugh. "I wonder what Blair thinks seeing it's just me."

"*Just* you, indeed. More like, *Wow, it's Mick*." She peered at the names inside the other ornament place cards. "Who are we with?"

"I recognize a few names. Nice people, but I expected to sit with the Underhills."

"I think they're at a family table. Dutch and Blair's dad are second cousins or something like that. Let's go say hi, though."

They got caught by acquaintances, however, and then the deejay called everyone to their seats. Their table filled quickly, and the wedding party was introduced to much fanfare. There was no gap between that and a prayer giving thanks for their evening meal.

Mick enjoyed the chicken piccata and light conversation at the table, but he couldn't help but sneak glances at Dutch and Beatie's table. Despite smiling and nodding, they both seemed strained. Were they upset about Mick showing up as Sadie's date? Or was Beatie feeling the effects of her fall more keenly as the day passed?

Maybe both. When Sadie finished her meal, he laid a hand on her arm. "Want to check in on Beatie and Dutch now?"

"That's a good idea. I feel like they're upset." She rose and placed her napkin on her chair. "I'm finally warm enough to take off your coat, though."

He hung it on the back of her chair, and with his hand at the small of her back, they navigated their way through the round tables across the room.

Halfway there, he spotted something green hanging from ribbon over the cake table. Something dangerous.

Mistletoe.

"Hey, Sadie, you did an excellent job with the decorations, but that parasitic plant isn't my favorite. Let's avoid standing over there."

She followed the direction of his gaze, then laughed. "Blair thought mistletoe would be cute in the cake-cutting photo. There are a few other bunches hanging around the room, too, and the staff here was kind enough to help me hang them this morning. Oh, there's Blair coming our way."

Blair, lovely in her white dress, hurried toward them, grinning widely. Sadie beamed at her friend. "Congratulations, Blair."

Mick gave the bride a gentle side hug. "Congratulations to you and Noah."

"Thanks." Blair stepped back and clasped her hands beneath her chin. "You two are so cute. You were even wearing Mick's coat, Sadie. Aww."

"Isn't he gallant, helping me out when I forgot mine? But speaking of cute, when Noah said his vows, it was so touching. Did you tear up? Because I sure did."

She had? Mick hadn't noticed.

But he *had* noticed how expertly Sadie diverted the conversation away from the two of them. She was a true diplomat, his Sadie.

"Yes, I did, but we can talk about all that later. Right now, you have something to do."

Sadie flinched. "Is there a problem with the toss bouquet? Is it Kelsey's headpiece again?"

"No, the flowers are great. You outdid yourself, and the Christmas roses are a huge hit. Several people have asked me about them, and I told them you have them at the farmstand."

"I'll order more tomorrow, then." Sadie's expression softened.

"That's not what you need to do." Blair lowered her head, like she was imitating a bull about to charge. "Tradition cannot be ignored, my friend."

She pointed up.

A bundle of mistletoe hung like a black cloud from the chandelier above their heads.

Mick grunted. Infernal parasitic plant.

Sadie's cheeks went pink. "We didn't mean to stand here."

"That makes it all the more fun." Blair fisted her hands at the waist of her white gown. "Don't be a spoilsport. Look at the audience you've generated."

Mick hadn't noticed until now how many pairs of eyes were fixed on them. A few of the groomsmen motioned for Mick to get on with it, and someone whistled at them.

"Everyone's looking at us," Sadie whispered to him.

He turned to face her so she would look at him, not the crowd. "You don't owe anyone anything, Sadie, and we don't have to do anything we don't want to do."

"I know." She paused while someone else whistled, this time sharper and louder. "But maybe we should. Just to make them shush. One quick kiss to appease the masses, and they'll have to leave us alone."

She had a point. "Are you sure?"

"I don't mind if you don't. If you do, then let's make a run for it." She licked her lips in a nervous gesture. "All in good fun, right?"

"Right."

So. They were doing this.

Kiss under the mistletoe.

He would give her the sort of quick peck he would give Beatie. No big deal.

He bent his head, and his lips barely grazed her cheek. There. Done.

"Boo," Blair shook her head. "Cheek kisses don't count."

"Says who?" Mick glanced at Sadie, but her expression was unreadable.

"Says tradition." Blair gestured at the crowd. "And all of us."

Mick wouldn't cave to peer pressure, but at someone's catcall, something in Sadie's eyes hardened.

"Kiss me, Larson."

He should say something lighthearted in response to her order, but words utterly failed him.

All he could do was reach out, gently lift her chin and obey her command.

Chapter Six

Don't make this weird.

The command zipped through Sadie's brain the moment Mick's thumb and forefinger touched her chin. *It will be over before you can count to one-one-thousand, and then you'll go on as if nothing happened.*

But he stared at her, so close that she could see flecks of gray in his eyes she'd never noticed before. And the moment Mick's lips touched hers, Sadie forgot to count to one.

She forgot everything except for the twin points of connection they shared, his fingers on her chin, his lips on hers. Warm, tender and so very nice, she didn't want the kiss to end. She leaned into him—

Oh, no, she couldn't do that. She pulled back, and only then did her ears unstop and she became aware of the *ooh*s and applause filling the room.

Heat rushed up her chest, neck and cheeks. The kiss had lasted more than the single second she'd anticipated. Long enough that she'd been lost to the world around her.

"What was it you told me when I suggested you bring Mick to the wedding? 'He and I are just friends'?" Blair made quotation marks with her fingers. "Friendship caught *fi-yah*." She stretched the word *fire* to two syllables.

"No, Blair." Sadie's voice cracked.

"I bought your act until that kiss." Blair's perfectly plucked eyebrows lowered in a stern expression. "And I have something important to say, so listen closely."

Dread pooled in Sadie's stomach.

"Thank you." Blair's features softened and she pulled Sadie into a hug. "You were so sweet to keep your relationship quiet, because you knew if you announced that you and Mick finally got together, no one would be talking about anything else for the rest of the reception. You didn't want to detract attention from me on my big day."

"I'd never want to diminish your wedding day. But that's not—"

"You told *us*, didn't you?" Beatie and Dutch appeared over Blair's shoulder. Dutch was grinning like a kid on Christmas morning, but Beatie was misty-eyed. Her words sounded blubbery, as if she was trying hard not to cry. "You said it was a *real* date."

"Among friends," Dutch added. "She said *friends*, honey."

"And we focused on the *friends* part, not the *real* part." Beatie's chin quivered. "And that's what true love is founded on. Friendship."

Wow, Sadie had really botched her explanations of Mick as her date if there were loopholes large enough for Blair, Beatie and Dutch to drive a truck through. "I'm sorry, but this is not what it looked like just now."

"I saw a kiss. Didn't you?" Beatie nudged Dutch in the ribs.

"We all saw it." Blair winked at Beatie. "My aunt is beckoning me. Talk to you later."

Sadie wished she could follow Blair out of the conversation. Out of the party. Out of the state.

Meanwhile, Mick was standing beside her, still and silent as a hunk of granite. Since he was no help, she pointed at the offending ball of greenery hanging from the chandelier. "We had to. We were under the mistletoe."

"Do tell." Dutch rocked on his heels, obviously not believing her explanation.

"It's a Christmas tradition. Going back a long time. Not as long as marshmallows, though, because they were invented by the ancient Egyptians. Right, Mick?" *Help me out here.*

Mick unfroze enough to nod. What was he agreeing to? Their kiss being non-romantic or the trivia about marshmallows?

Say something. It wasn't like their teeny tiny kiss could have rendered him speechless.

"I know why you were so coy." Beatie wagged a finger at them. "You wanted some time to enjoy your new relationship without everyone sticking their noses in it. Dutch and I were the same way."

"Beatie—"

"We won't pester you now, but we told you that you should be together, didn't we?"

"We did." Dutch took his wife's arm. "Let's get you off your feet now. Come on, honey."

Mick grabbed Sadie's hand and pulled her toward the exit. "Let's get some air while we can."

"Oh, *now* you're able to talk?"

"What?" He looked back at her.

"Never mind." Too many people were watching them with approving smiles.

He pushed open the door to the courtyard and led her out into the brisk, clear night. She clung to his hand as he drew her to a darker corner opposite the ballroom. "Mick, what are we going to do? Beatie is so happy she's weeping."

Probably because Sadie was such a desperate case that she thought this day would never happen.

"I saw."

"Then why are we outside? We have to go back and make them understand the truth."

"And make an even bigger scene?" He stopped walking now that they were as far away as they could get without leaving the site. "Let's take a minute and talk this through."

"What's there to talk through? They think—"

"I know, but you're hardly breathing, and I don't want you to panic. Take a long breath—in through your nose, out through your mouth."

"I don't want to breathe. I want to set the record straight."

"We will, but neither of us are in the right headspace for a rational conversation with them at this exact moment." Mick stood in front of her. "Look at me. Deep breath."

Fine. She met his gaze and took a long, steady breath through her nose. The cold air stung her nostrils, but her heart rate slowed a fraction. She took another breath in sync with Mick.

He'd been right. She needed those deep breaths.

"Okay, I'm better now." One more breath. She shuddered as she exhaled.

"What was I thinking, dragging you out here without a jacket?" Mick rubbed her arms with his large hands. "You must be freezing."

"I was in such a tizzy I didn't notice." But it was warmer with his hands on her arms. "You were right, though. I was a little overwhelmed back there. You were, too, Mr. Deer-in-the-Headlights. Why didn't you say anything?"

"I didn't expect—I was caught off guard. And then they weren't listening. There's no use pleading your case if the other person refuses to hear it."

"So how do we clear this up, short of stealing the mic from the deejay to announce to everyone we aren't dating?"

Mick chuckled. "That's probably not the sort of reception memory that Blair and Noah had in mind. It'll all sort out, Sadie."

"With Blair, sure. I can text her later to set her straight. But Dutch and Beatie need to hear the truth sooner than later."

"Agreed, but in private. Why don't I go in and invite them out here to talk? On my way out, I'll grab your jacket."

"You mean *your* jacket." She might very well cover her head with it so she could hide for the rest of the evening.

"Mick, Sadie? Don't mean to interrupt."

She spun around. Dutch stood across the courtyard, looking hesitant. But it was perfect timing. "No interruption at all." Sadie peered over his shoulder. "Is Beatie with you?"

"No." Dutch looked around as if afraid of being overheard, but there was no one else outside. All was quiet, except for the faint strains of conversation and the thumping bass of the music spilling from the ballroom. "I wanted to talk to you two alone. About Beatie."

Wait, hadn't he said something about Beatie needing to get off her feet a few minutes ago? What was that about? Anxiety pooled in her stomach. "What's wrong?"

Dutch let out a tired sigh. "Beatie doesn't want anyone to know, so please keep this confidential. She's had a few incidents with her balance. Misjudging where things are, falling into things."

A memory flooded Sadie's brain. "The week before Thanksgiving, when Blair and I were planning the flowers, Beatie stumbled into the picnic bench. That wasn't a one-time thing?"

"No. She's fallen other times. Including today." Dutch glanced at Mick. "As you know."

He did? He hadn't told her. Sadie wrapped her arms around her torso.

Mick let out a sigh. "I didn't realize it was a pattern, but now I understand why she reacted so strongly against the idea of visiting the ER. She's been already?"

"Yep. The worst fall was on Thanksgiving, at her sister's. Shook her up real good. That finally got her to agree to see a doctor. Things progressed from there, and she sees a specialist on Tuesday. We know something's wrong, but we don't know what it is yet."

"Oh, Dutch." Sadie knew better than to speculate about the possible medical conditions that could cause Beatie to fall, but it was difficult to keep those scary thoughts at bay. "How awful."

"The wait for tests and results can be excruciating." Mick shook his head. "How are you both holding up?"

"She's been down about it, but that's what I came out to tell you—you two dating is the first thing that's made her happy in weeks. You've given her quite a boost."

"But—" Sadie couldn't finish. How could she blurt out the truth now?

Mick didn't say anything, either, but at least he'd lost the shocked-deer expression.

Then he squeezed Dutch's shoulder. "Beatie might not want anyone to know, but we still want to support you—both of you—however you need. How can we help? Prayer, of course, but could you benefit from some meals?"

"Prayer is all for now. We know God is with us. No matter what storms we face, we're determined to focus on Him and His blessings. Like you two. It's always a happy thing when two wonderful people find each other. I can't thank you enough for giving Beatie something joyful to focus on. Now, I'll let you two lovebirds be, and go back to my sweetheart." He winked. "But don't stay out too long."

Neither she nor Mick moved an inch after Dutch left, fixed to their spots like flagpoles. Then Mick let out a long breath. "Poor Beatie. But I couldn't tell Dutch the truth about us after he told us she could be sick. The words froze on my tongue."

"Same here." Sadie's stomach swirled with so many emotions she couldn't name them all.

"What if…what if we let them continue to think we're dating? Just for a while?"

He couldn't be serious. "How long is a while?"

"Until she's in a better place. She should have answers by Christmas, and after that, we can tell them we're just friends."

As tempted as Sadie was to avoid hurting Beatie, she wasn't sure she could agree to this. "It feels like fibbing."

"I get that."

"But this made her happy. And she's probably so scared right now."

"Would you be willing if it didn't mean lying?" Mick's expression was impossible to read.

Her words turned to gurgles in her throat. "What?"

"Maybe we should just date. For December, or until Beatie has a diagnosis and is in a better place. Whichever comes first. But our grand romance can be over by the new year."

"If our relationship has a predetermined expiration date, then it's not real."

"Depends on how you define *dating*. We'd be two people spending time together and not dating anyone else. No one else has to know there's no romance involved."

"And it would make Beatie smile." She put her hands to her lips, certain there would be no repeats of the mistletoe mishap they'd just shared—the better to keep her thoughts and feelings for Mick firmly in the friend zone.

But at the same time? "It would be nice to have a... plus-one to events."

"Like this one."

"And we like to hang out together anyway." She couldn't think straight, but she couldn't deny she wanted to make Beatie smile. "Maybe...pretending through December wouldn't be so bad."

"So, we're doing this?"

"We're doing this."

He wrapped his arm around her again. "Let's get you warm. What kind of fake boyfriend am I to keep you out in this cold?"

Walking inside, she gulped.

Mick had the biggest heart of any man she knew. He said yes to anyone and everyone in need, whether animal or human. Like Wade and his nativity project. Or Sadie, whose friendship had put him in this pickle.

He loved God and served in church and the community. He was compassionate and loyal and sacrificial in his giving. As long as she lived, she would never find another man like Mick—would she?

And now he was hers.

At least for the month of December. And then she would have to give him back and return to the way things were.

Their friendship was nothing to sneeze at. But for the briefest of moments, she allowed herself to wish she was really dating someone. Her someone.

She would not allow herself to wish that man was Mick.

Gossip spread through Goldenrod like pollen on a spring breeze, and Mick found it equally irritating. In the two days since Blair and Noah's wedding, the news about Mick and Sadie being a so-called item had reached Glenda, who was so happy she hugged him when he walked into the clinic this morning.

A few pet owners had brought it up during appointments too. Couldn't a guy just work without talking about his fake love life? He did his best to answer truthfully that he loved hanging out with Sadie, because he didn't want to dishonor Sadie or God. Who knew trying to make a sick friend feel happy could be so complicated?

At least the day was almost over. He left Exam Room 1 and the nosy owner of a Siberian husky pup, and braced himself for whoever was in Exam Room 2, his final patient of the day. The notes scribbled on the paperwork in the wall-mounted document holder, however, made him forget about the town's wagging tongues.

"Alex." He shook hands with the worried-looking man around his age. Alex Callahan was a relative newcomer to Goldenrod, having moved here after going into the cabin kit–building business with Wyatt. Mick glanced at Alex's black-and-white mutt, Molly, resting on the exam table as he moved to the sink to wash up. "I see Molly was here last week and saw Dr. Coggins. She swallowed a fitness tracker?"

"Yeah, my mom's tracker fell next to Molly's dish. I tried to stop her, but she was too fast. She gobbles everything, left over from her time on the streets, I guess. Anyway, she threw it up, like the other vet—Coggins—said she would." Alex ruffled his coppery hair. "But she's lethargic and doesn't want to eat."

Mick dried his hands. He trusted Leonard Coggins to have given Molly appropriate care, but it was clear something still wasn't right. "Was the tracker intact? Do you still have it?" Hopefully the battery hadn't leaked.

Alex grimaced. "My mom ordered a new one, so I took it to the e-waste drop-off at the tech store, but it was in one piece. No toothmarks or anything."

"That's good." Mick checked the ancient computer in the exam room, which still hadn't uploaded Molly's X-ray from her visit last week. The test could reveal another possible culprit for Molly's malaise, something his clinic partner might have missed—if only the file would load.

Swallowing down his annoyance with the outdated technology in the office, he began his examination. Molly's fluffy tail gave a little thump when he rubbed her neck.

"You're such a sweetheart," he told her. And a mystery. When she'd wandered into Alex's yard two weeks ago, Mick had given her a thorough examination, including scanning her for a microchip that could identify her owners. She didn't have one, though. Nor had anyone responded to the Found Dog notifications Alex had placed on a local neighborhood app.

Alex had chosen to call her Molly and keep her until her owners were found rather than leave her at the overcrowded shelter. Mick had set Alex up with food, toys and advice about getting her fixed if he ultimately decided to keep her as his own. But neither of them had anticipated Molly would have such an eventful two weeks.

Mick listened to her lungs and heart, which were both healthy, although her heart rate was a little fast. Then he gently ran his hand down Molly's side, searching for swelling. When he reached beneath her, her abdomen felt firmer than it had when he'd examined her a few weeks ago. He guided the compliant dog onto her side so he could better assess her.

And then all became clear. "I don't think Molly is suffering from tangling with your mom's Fitbit. She's pregnant."

"P—what?" Alex's lips parted with a pop.

"Only a few weeks along. She must have conceived right before finding her way into your yard."

"She had an X-ray last week." Alex looked like he'd been struck in the gut. "Wouldn't it have shown that?"

"Not necessarily that early." Mick scratched Molly's floppy ears. "Alex, Molly had been on her own for a while when she found you, and at this point, I would be surprised if someone claims her. But she needs a home, and puppies are more than you bargained for when you rescued her. If it's too much, I can find a foster home for her."

"I have a feeling that foster home would be yours." Alex's lips twitched. "Wyatt says you're always taking in strays and finding homes for them. You set him up with his dog, Ranger, right?"

"It was more that Ranger and Wyatt found each other." But Mick was not having that sort of success with placing Gidget, the miniature horse, despite multiple attempts. According to the agencies he'd spoken to, she was too close to retirement age to place, but she had a lot of love to give. Even if she didn't function in a service capacity anymore, she would thrive as a helping companion.

Mick had to trust God to provide a place for Gidget, and in the meantime, she was getting along well with Wyatt's mares and the humans at Foxtail Farm.

Molly seemed happy with Alex, too, but now that she was expecting puppies? "I promise that wherever she goes—with me or another foster—she'll be cared for and loved."

"No need." Alex rubbed Molly's neck with both hands as the dog looked up at him with adoring brown eyes. "I have no experience with puppies, but I'm willing to learn. For Molly."

"I'll be with you every step of the way, and when the pups are old enough, I'll help you find homes for them."

No way would Mick allow Molly's litter to end up like their mama, fending for herself in the cold until someone found her and brought her inside.

It was another reminder of how much the community could use Wade Gibbons's donation to expand the animal shelter, which he was offering in exchange for the living nativity…for which Mick had a meeting tonight. He glanced at his watch.

"Late for a date with Sadie, Doc?"

Alex had obviously heard about the mistletoe kiss. Who hadn't? At least Mick and Sadie had had the forethought to text her sisters, Wyatt and Thatcher before they'd left the wedding reception that they'd decided to "date" for December. They didn't betray Dutch and Beatie's confidence, but asked their families to trust them and go with it until January.

In response, they'd received an immediate flurry of incredulous texts that questioned their judgment, but their families had ultimately accepted it.

"No date tonight. Living-nativity meeting." Mick finished jotting down notes, ready to change the subject. "Are you going to be able to make it to the event?"

"It's on my calendar. Some of my family is visiting me then, so they'll come too. My mom, aunt and uncle—he's a veterinarian, just like you. His practice is doing so well that they've been able to partner with a local shelter. You two would have a lot to talk about."

"I'd love to. I can use all the help I can get." Because without Wade's donation, there would be no help for the shelter in Goldenrod. Mick wouldn't mind talking about vet practices, either, because his goals to improve the clinic weren't just stalled—they were floundering.

But Alex didn't need to hear about that. "Sounds like your uncle can help you with puppy questions, too, but for now, let's schedule a follow-up appointment for Molly."

Their conversation remained on the safe, Sadie-free topic of canine prenatal care through the rest of the visit, until Mick escorted Alex and Molly out of the exam room.

No patients were in the lobby, but Mick's partner, Leonard, a spare man with square glasses and thinning white hair, stood behind Glenda at her desk and stared at her computer monitor. "Now hit the Escape key."

"I did, Leonard, but something's not working—oh, excuse us." Glenda's frown smoothed at the sight of a customer with a credit card in his hand. "Mr. Callahan, I'm so sorry, but the computer is acting fussy. I can't pull up your file, which means I can't link it to a credit card. May I send you a bill for today's visit?"

Mick forced himself not to grimace. If this sort of thing happened every so often, okay, but it was becoming the norm at the clinic. "That means we can't yet schedule Molly's next appointment, Alex. Sorry for the inconvenience."

"No worries." Alex slipped his credit card back into his wallet. "I'll call tomorrow about her follow-up."

Once Alex and Molly left, Glenda grabbed her purse from the drawer beside her chair. "Shall I turn off the computer, or do you two want to fuss with it?"

"Go ahead and turn it off." Mick straightened a bag of dog food on a display shelf. "I'll run a scan in the morning."

Glenda pulled her keys from her purse with a jingling sound. "I'll lock the front door behind me, then. See you tonight, Mick?"

"You've got it, Glenda." Mick switched off the office lights.

"Do you two have a church meeting?" Leonard stripped off his white coat as he led Mick back into the hall toward their offices.

"It's our first on-site rehearsal for the living nativity at Foxtail Farm. Glenda is in the cast." Mick shoved his hands in his coat pockets. "About the computer, Leonard?"

"If this is about Mr. Callahan being billed, he didn't seem to mind."

"This sort of thing has been happening more and more frequently, though. I couldn't load Molly's X-rays either. It's a different system, but the point stands. We need to update things around here for our patients' sakes as well as our own."

"It's a lot of money, Mick, and I'm too old of a dog to learn new tricks." Leonard chuckled as he ducked into his office and grabbed his black leather bag. "The practice will be yours soon enough, and you can implement whatever changes you wish."

Soon enough? "You're planning to retire, Leonard?"

"Oh, in five years or so."

"That's too long to go without new computers and billing software."

"Money doesn't grow on trees, Mick."

"But sometimes you have to spend some to invest in the future." It was a delicate balance.

"I have to run, Mick, but it sounds like you do too. See you tomorrow."

Frustrated, Mick bid him good night. Then he drove home and gobbled down reheated lasagna while Fly ate her evening meal before he shrugged back into his coat. With

Fly beside him in the truck and Christmas carols playing on the radio, he drove to Foxtail Farm.

The farmstand was closed for the day, and without activity, it was difficult to tell where the apple orchard ended and the inky sky began. Thankfully, the familiar path to the stable was well-lit. He slipped a hot pink halter with a matching lead onto Gidget. She and Fly walked back with him to the farmstand, side by side, like pals in line at kindergarten.

It reinforced that Gidget wasn't just comfortable with other animals. She liked them, and she would be so much happier in a home.

Lord, who do You have in mind for Gidget? I trust You to work this out in Your time, but help me to be patient.

He could use some patience at work, too, but on days like this, when the computers didn't cooperate and Leonard didn't seem to want to invest in the business or their patients, Mick wondered what his life would have been like if he hadn't promised Grandpa Hank he would stay in Goldenrod and help run the clinic.

But as Sadie came into view, adjusting a waterproof red bow on the John Deere, he reminded himself that even when things weren't as he wanted them to be, it was a blessing to know where he stood. At work. With Aunt Jillian and Uncle Gary.

And with Sadie. His date for December.

She wore jeans, a burgundy turtleneck and a striped beanie with a pompom on top. Cute, but hardly warm enough for the night's temperatures. "Hey," he called. "What do you have against coats?"

Grinning, she abandoned the bow to rush toward him. "Nothing, my coat's hanging on the tractor. Well, hello, ladies." Each of her hands patted an animal. Fly's yellow tail wagged so hard it thumped Mick's leg. "Are Gidget and Fly joining us for rehearsal?"

"I thought they'd enjoy it. Gidget is used to being around people."

"She'll be a hit." Sadie snapped her fingers. "That reminds me, did you find enough animals for the nativity?"

"Sure did. Sheep, goats, Ike the camel and, of course, Clover the donkey."

They walked toward the empty area by the parking lot where the nativity trail would begin, pausing for her to grab her puffy beige coat. "The animals are done, but the decorations aren't. I'd like to add luminaria at the end of the nativity, lining the path our guests will walk to the farmstand. It's more for ambience than lighting, since the path is well-lit, but I think it would be pretty and it wouldn't cost much to do."

"Luminaria? Do you mean those brown paper lunch bags lit up by candles?"

"Weighed down by sand, yes. We can use battery-powered votive candles."

He tried to envision it while they walked, gravel crunching beneath their feet, Gidget's small, warm body brushing his legs. "Sounds nice. We can make a party of putting them together."

"Speaking of parties." Her tone sounded doomed. "Since last night, you and I have been invited to a few events."

"I didn't get invited to anything. That I know of." He hadn't checked his email since leaving work.

"Since we're *dating,* I received the invitations for both of us."

"Ah. What sort of events?"

"The Christmas parade with my Bible study group on Thursday, Foxtail staff party Friday, a cookie exchange next

Monday at Blair's, since they'll be back from their brief honeymoon and want their friends to see their new apartment. Then there's caroling with my Bible study group next Tuesday, and of course, Wyatt and Natalie's Christmas Eve party before church. And Pastor Luke asked if you and I would chaperone the youth group sledding on Saturday—because we're supposed to get snow later in the week—and he wanted to make sure we're coming to the kids' pageant Sunday night. We don't have to say yes to anything, of course."

"I want to. If you do, that is. But my brain is short-circuiting from all these details." He pulled out his phone and opened the calendar. "Thursday and Monday are clear. You're already invited to my aunt and uncle's open house at the ranch next Wednesday, and the Holiday 'Paw-ty' for the animal shelter next Thursday, but we should probably attend those together." For Beatie's sake, of course.

"Sounds good. Wow, if you count Blair's wedding, we will have a dozen dates this month. That's almost a song." She began humming "The Twelve Days of Christmas."

"Three staff parties, two church kids' events and a partridge in a pear tree," he sang.

"I'm looking forward to them all. Except for the pear-tree part. We're Team Apple at Foxtail Farm."

Gidget made a snuffling sound as if she agreed.

"Partridge in an apple tree, then. Regardless, we'll have a fun December."

"A busy December," she amended. "I'll be on more dates in the next two and a half weeks than I've had in the past two and a half years."

"Double that amount of time since I last had a date."

But he couldn't say the same about a kiss, since he and Sadie met beneath the mistletoe two days ago. He had refused to think about it since it happened, when he'd been unable to form a coherent thought for a solid five minutes afterward. There was no good answer for why he'd gone into instant shock.

No safe answer, anyway.

He couldn't allow those thoughts to continue. He and Sadie were friends. Love and marriage were not in his future.

But just because his arrangement with Sadie was temporary didn't mean he couldn't enjoy it.

Mick turned to see the first of a stream of cars turning into the Foxtail parking lot. "Time for the first nativity rehearsal. Are you ready?"

"For that, yes. For people to bug us about being a couple?" Sadie cringed.

"Don't worry. I've got you." He took her hand, because Beatie and Dutch would be at the rehearsal. But also because he wanted to. He would never know what real love was like, but maybe this December he could have a glimpse of what might have been, were he the sort of person who could be loved.

Chapter Seven

Ten minutes later, Sadie stood atop a hay bale and offered instructions to the volunteers gathered in the wide, empty space where the nativity walkthrough would begin once the sets were in place.

"And lastly, thank you one and all for everything you're doing to make the living nativity an unforgettable experience for our town. Now, we can break into our groups—oh, yes, Robin?"

Robin Pacheco, the drama teacher, flicked her long gray-streaked hair over her shoulder and climbed onto the hay bale beside her. "May I say something from on high, the better to be heard?"

"Of course." Sadie started to step down, only for Mick to offer his hand to her. Even though they both wore gloves, a jolt shot up her arm.

No, no, no. Mick was just being nice. If it looked like a gallant gesture to Beatie, all the better, but you cannot respond like an idiot every time Mick touches you.

Since the kiss, however, she had struggled to balance the good parts of fake-dating her best friend with the inherent dangers of it. To enjoy time with him and the fun of having a plus-one while not reawakening her long-buried attraction to him.

If that were even possible, now that they'd kissed. *Get a grip, Dalton.*

Robin smiled at the gathering. "You are all invited to the production of *A Christmas Carol* at the high school tomorrow night. Each of my students here tonight will be performing, and we would love to see you. Curtain is at seven. Now that I've made my pitch, I'd appreciate if the cast could begin breaking into groups as Sadie said—shepherds by that big tree, angel choir right here. Magi, innkeepers, Mary and Joseph? Follow me."

Ike the camel's owner, Leroy, would play one of the wise men, but the other two were from Robin's adult drama class. Dutch and Beatie had been chosen to be the innkeepers, and a young married couple volunteered to portray Mary and Joseph. As the actors wandered off, Sadie spied Kelsey sidling up to Juniper Jones, the nine-year-old foster daughter of Foxtail's new bookkeeper, Bliss Anderson. Never without Coco, her black Labrador epilepsy-alert dog, Juniper was patting Gidget, who was standing with Beatie. Since Beatie needed to move on, Kelsey spoke to Juniper, then gently ushered her to join the other members of the angel choir.

Mick followed the direction of her gaze. "Is something up with the angels?"

"No, I'm just noting how gifted Kelsey is with children. Look at how well she engages the younger ones. No matter what she does in life or where she goes, that gift will be a blessing." Sadie would have to make a point of thanking her for her help. She hadn't forgotten that Kelsey had harbored some insecurities at Blair's wedding.

"I can see that. She's a good kid, and you're right, that's a gift." He smiled down at her. "Right now, though, I'm particularly grateful for your gift of event planning."

Her? "No way. Organization is Natalie's gift, not mine."

"I'd say you have it, too, Sadie. But I also appreciate the way you say yes every time I ask for help with events to benefit the animal shelter, without hesitation. And you make everything look so much better because you have an eye for flow and beauty. And you think about things like theme, which never occurs to me."

"That's true," she teased, but it was true. She had been through enough animal-shelter fundraisers with him to know the man did not know how to run with a motif.

Which made her wonder...was she squeezing everything out of this event's theme? She stared at the scene in front of her. Hard.

Jillian addressed her group of designers on the placement of the simple wood-framed sets they were constructing. Wyatt gathered the parking attendants and Thatcher unloaded bales of straw for the animals from the back of his truck while Robin addressed the cast. Sadie's gaze cut through the chaos of a first group rehearsal, through the lack of finished scenery or costumes, and then it became clear.

Mick bumped her shoulder with his. "I recognize that expression. You're in the decorating zone."

He knew her well, didn't he? "Your aunt's plans for the individual sets are great, but I think we're neglecting the in-between spaces. The entrance and exit. The path itself."

"I thought you wanted luminaria for the path."

"The path from the nativity's exit to the farmstand, yes. It's a visual clue that joins the past to the present. But throughout the living nativity, while guests are walking from set to set? We ought to dress those areas to keep the spirit of the experience unbroken."

"Got it. What do you need?"

"To start? Straw."

"I know just the man to ask. Hey, Thatcher?"

Her cousin hopped down from the back of his truck, bits of straw adhering to his jacket. "What do you two *lovebirds* need?"

They weren't lovebirds and he knew it, even if he didn't understand all the reasons why. "I'm ignoring that saucy remark, Thatcher, because I'm hoping there's more straw at the ranch we can use."

His dark brows pulled low. "You need more animal bedding than this?"

"No, I want to offer bales as seating along the way in case a guest needs to rest, and I think bundles of straw would make a good prop." Sadie swept her hand over what would become the entrance area. "This should be like a gateway, so when guests pass into the experience, the world around them looks—feels—biblical in setting. Not that we can re-create a two-thousand-year-old Judean village in a California apple orchard, but we can add to the ambience."

Mick made a humming noise of agreement. "What else do you have in mind?"

"Rustic-looking pots, maybe some cooking utensils and ancient-looking carpentry tools. Fabric tents in the meadow, with lamps inside them. Fake flames, of course, for safety. More flameless lanterns along the path would add to the atmosphere too. Ooh, so would scent. What if we had a few essential-oil diffusers with frankincense and myrrh in the Magi scene?" She started tapping notes into her phone. "And a Christmas star. That gold foil star on a pole isn't doing it for me. The Magi were drawn by the star's light. Light is what we need."

Thatcher snorted. "I can help with a lot of that, but you'll have to talk to NASA about the star."

"Dude, I think she's talking about a light bulb." Mick looked at her. "Right?"

"Yes. A single bright light. Don't you think it would be pretty to have a beam of brilliant white starlight shining into the stable? Maybe through the window, dispersed through a curtain?"

"Are curtains historically accurate for biblical times?" Thatcher's tongue was firmly in his cheek. "I think we'd better halt production until we do more research."

Mick's teasing grin pulled higher on the left. "It's not like we're in a hurry or anything."

Was this what having brothers was like? Nonstop teasing?

Although her kiss with Mick had not been the least bit brotherly. The unwelcome reminder sent a hot blush up her neck.

"You two are so annoying." Sadie stepped away before they noticed. "I'm going to talk to Jillian about a *curtain*."

Their chuckles followed her into the chilly night. As she walked, her hasty online search revealed houses in ancient Israel could have had shutters, but she hadn't found anything yet about curtains. Oh well. This one would, if only to spite Thatcher.

And Mick, of course.

Their teasing was enough to give a gal a headache. She rubbed the spot on the right side of her forehead, willing it to be gone. Within five minutes, though, it became clear this was no ordinary headache.

She found Mick and Thatcher again. "I've got a migraine coming on. I need to go home for my medication."

Mick was at her side in an instant. "I'll walk you there."

"Get some sleep, Sadie." Thatcher frowned. "I'll fill everyone in."

"Thanks, cuz. But, Mick, it's so close—you don't need to come with me."

"*You* might not need me, but I need to make sure you're home safe, okay?"

"Very date-like."

"Very *friend-like*," he countered as they started up the path around the farmstand and through the rental-cabin area to the farmhouse.

He hadn't whistled for Fly, but the dog suddenly appeared at Sadie's side, trotting to match their pace. "Aww, poor girl must have thought you were leaving without her, Mick."

"Actually, I think she's worried about you." Mick pushed aside a low-hanging branch on the path. "She's walking with you, not me."

Sure enough, Fly looked up at Sadie with large, dark eyes. "That's sweet, but why? She's your baby, not mine, and she's not a therapy dog."

"No, but she's intuitive and she's accustomed to you. She clearly senses you're not feeling great."

"What a good girl." If bending down didn't carry the risk of causing her migraine-related nausea, Sadie would have given Fly a good rubdown.

They cleared a cluster of trees and strode up the cement walkway to the white ranch-style house. White fairy lights hung from the eaves, and multicolored mini lights netted the evergreen shrubs planted in front of the brick foundation, illuminating their path up three steps to the porch. She pulled her keys from her purse.

Mick took the keys from her and unlocked the door. "Shall I make you a mug of tea?"

"I'm good, thanks." Although she had to admit, the idea of being married and having someone take care of her at times like these sounded wonderful. She pushed open the door, and Fly strutted right on in.

"Come, Fly." Mick retreated down the porch steps. "Sadie needs to go to bed."

Fly didn't budge from her spot in the foyer, where she stared up at Sadie.

Sadie unwound her scarf from her neck. "Don't you want to go home, girl?"

"I don't think she does. She wants to be with you."

"That can't be right." Sadie crossed the foyer and opened the door to her private quarters. Fly trotted in like she owned the place.

Mick shrugged. "I think she wants to stay the night. Are you up for it?"

"I'm touched she wants to take care of me. Are you sure you don't mind?"

"Not at all. Do you have something I can use for a water dish?"

She directed him to the cabinet beside the stove where she kept a stash of bowls. She filled a glass of water for herself and took it to the bathroom, where she found her over-the-counter medication. When she'd finished, Fly was in the doorway, watching her.

Mick waited in the kitchen. "I'll be back in the morning for her. And to check on you. Good night to my two favorite ladies. Praying you feel better fast, Sadie."

"Thanks. Good night, Mick."

Once he was gone, she made quick work of cleaning up, and soon she and Fly were snuggled together in Sadie's bed. Sleep would be beneficial, but her thoughts were still racing with details for the nativity. She might as well order that gauze for the curtain while it was on her mind.

She got out of bed and returned with her laptop, balancing it on her knees. Thankfully, she wasn't experiencing vision issues from her headache, so it didn't bother her to get online and purchase the fabric.

Before she was finished, Fly had started to snooze.

Sadie wasn't quite ready to join Fly in dreamland, though. She might as well take care of other business. She wouldn't have time to go down the mountain to the flower market over the next few weeks, and the farmstand could do with a few more poinsettias, which were often sold as last-minute gifts in the days leading up to Christmas.

She logged on to the site of her favorite floral distributor that made deliveries this way. It didn't take long to add poinsettias to the cart, some with red bracts, some pink and some white. But as she did so, a variety called Jingle Bell Rock appeared on the side of her screen as a shopping suggestion. The pretty white bracts with red edges were gorgeous, and the name alone might inspire a farmstand shopper to purchase it.

She added some to the cart.

The addition must have affected some algorithms, because her screen filled with some of the most interesting poinsettias she had ever seen. While she knew they came in various warm tones, she had never seen one so bright an orange. Or so soft an apricot or lovely a yellow…

They weren't typical holiday colors, but they reminded Sadie of Life Savers and gumdrops. Like…candies on a gingerbread house.

Did I just find next year's decor theme for the farmstand?

She yawned wide and long like a cat. It was time to sleep, but what if she forgot her gingerbread-house idea tomorrow, in the busyness of everything else?

She added the poinsettias to the cart, wonderfully named plants like Marco Polo, Lemon Glow and Ice Punch. But if she were going to decorate the whole farmstand with them, she would need scores. Maybe a few hundred. How much would that cost?

She increased the quantities just to see the calculated cost. Yikes. She'd have to budget all year for that.

She shifted the interesting varieties from her shopping cart to "Save for Later" so they would be in her account next time she got on the site. Now she was in no danger of forgetting her idea. The cart reflected a much more acceptable price once again. "Much better."

Fly lifted her sleepy head, and Sadie patted her between her soft ears. "Sorry, girl, I didn't mean to wake you."

Fly peered at Sadie, and apparently judging her to be okay, she got up and spun in a half circle, stepping on the laptop in the process.

The screen changed, and Sadie had a moment of panic. But phew, there was her name, and the credit card information was ready to go. Sadie hit the "Order Now" button, shut the laptop, set it on her bedside table and turned out the light.

Next thing she knew, pale light was streaming through the window. She must have fallen asleep. Fly rested at her feet, and her phone was buzzing.

Several text messages from Mick lit up the screen, each of them sent a half hour apart. "Looks like your dad has been texting us for a while, Fly."

Are you up? How are you feeling?

I guess you're sleeping in. Text when you're up.

Hey, I've got breakfast for you two. Dropping them off at your apartment door. Thatcher told me where to find the key to the main house. By the way, you really shouldn't hide a house key beneath the potted plant on the porch. First place thieves look.

He had just sent the last message, so she had time to change and run a brush through her hair before he arrived. She met him in the foyer, and he carried in the morning cold, along with a white bag smelling of coffee and a breakfast sandwich.

While Fly trotted past them outside, Mick offered the bag. "Croissant. Your favorite."

"Thank you. Come in?"

"No thanks, I'll take Fly and go. I've got patients coming to the clinic soon. Feeling better?"

"Much. It was so nice to have a slumber party with Fly too." Her stomach rumbled, ready for the ham-and-egg croissant. "I'll be good to go to *A Christmas Carol* tonight."

"If you're sure. Do you know what triggered the migraine?"

"It could've been fatigue, but maybe cold. Ice on my skin has done it before, and it's not quite the same, but last night my ears got cold. Who knows."

"I'm just glad you're better." Mick's tender gaze made her knees knock. Then he opened the door to leave. "Don't overdo it today, okay?"

"Okay." But that was an impossible thing to promise. There was so much to do before Christmas, in so little time…

And yet all she could think about at this moment was how drawn to him she felt.

She mustn't forget this thing between her and Mick wasn't real. It was pretend.

But it didn't feel that way. Not in her heart, not in her bones. Was he affected by their kiss, too?

Don't go there. For both of your sakes.

She sat down to her croissant sandwich breakfast and opened her Bible. There was too much going on, in her circumstances as well as her heart, not to begin the day with prayer.

* * *

On the fourth date of Christmas...

Mick hummed along to the old carol as he and Fly followed the mouthwatering aroma of barbecue around Foxtail's farmstand on Friday night—his and Sadie's fourth date in less than a week.

Their first date was Blair's wedding. Seeing *A Christmas Carol* at the high school on Tuesday was the second. Last night, Thursday, they'd gone downtown for the holiday parade.

When December ended, he would miss having Sadie as his automatic partner for events like this, but at least he wouldn't lose her altogether. Her unchanging friendship was reliable, and he wouldn't trade it for anything.

She might trade him in, however, since he was over an hour late to the Foxtail staff holiday party.

He rounded the farmstand to the clearing where Foxtail's rental cabin stood, sparkling with lights. The night might be crisp and cloudy, with a forecast of snow later, but the scene before him of people gathered around a blaze in the firepit was warm and welcoming.

Sadie, bundled up in a red knit cap with a pompom on top and a thick scarf to match, rushed to meet him. "You made it."

"Sorry I'm late."

"Don't be silly. Emergency surgery takes precedence over parties." She bent to greet Fly, rubbing his dog with both of her hands. Then she glanced at Mick. "I'm so sorry that stray dog got hit by a car. How is he?"

"The impact wasn't bad, but it was rough. Not because of his injuries, but because the clinic was dangerously low in certain supplies. Apparently, the computer crashed while Leonard was ordering them, and he didn't check to ensure the order went through." His voice was low, but he instantly felt remorse. "Sorry, I shouldn't have said anything."

"You've got to let off steam, and I'm a safe person. How can I pray for you if I don't know what's going on in your life?"

"I could use prayers for patience."

"And new computers." She shuddered. "I can't imagine how frustrating that must have been, but it sounds like you made do."

"With God's help." And he was comforted knowing Wade's check for the animal shelter would clear after the nativity, so soon there would be fewer strays on the streets.

Fly wasn't the only animal in attendance tonight. Two Labrador Retrievers rested beside their owners at the firepit—Wyatt's chocolate, Ranger, and young Juniper's black, Coco—both two of his favorite patients. Even Gidget was here, standing beside Beatie. "Thanks for including Gidget."

"We all adore her. Still no word of a home for her?"

"Not yet." He lowered his voice. "Any news on Beatie?" It hadn't even been a week since Blair's wedding, but it was possible she could have had some results.

"Not a word, I'm afraid. I think her appointment was rescheduled."

"We'll keep praying."

The jangling clang of a triangle drew their attention to the cabin, where Natalie stood on the porch. "Come on over, everyone! Time to eat!"

Mick rubbed his stomach as Thatcher pulled up alongside them for the short walk. "I got here just in time."

"I'll say. We played Christmas charades before you got here." Thatcher rolled his eyes.

"It wasn't that bad." Bliss, Juniper's foster mom, gave

Thatcher's shoulder a consoling pat. "You were a very nice reindeer."

Juniper shook her head. "I thought you were a rabbit, Mr. Dalton, with your hands like long ears over your head."

Thatcher laughed. "Those were supposed to be my antlers."

The conversation was full of good-natured ribbing and merry laughter as Foxtail's employees and their families loaded their plates and found comfortable seating, either inside the cabin or around the firepit. Mick took Sadie's plate for her so she could carry their mugs of hot apple cider. "Do you want to eat inside or out?"

"Out."

He liked her choice. They settled against the plump cushions of a wicker love seat near the firepit and balanced their plates on their knees.

The Daltons had outdone themselves. Barbecued tri-tip beef, roasted potatoes, Sadie's apple-cider baked beans, and salad comprised of greens, thin slices of apple, pecans and feta cheese battled for room on his plate.

Sadie scooped a forkful of beans. "Is this like your staff parties at the vet clinic?"

Mick swallowed a bite of tender beef. "In some ways. We close the office for a catered lunch for the techs and assistants, but we definitely do not play charades." Leonard's idea of a festively decorated lobby was a banner that said, "Best Wishes *fur* a Merry Christmas."

"We might be stuck playing charades tomorrow if we don't get snow before the youth group sledding party."

"It's definitely cold enough." He set his mug on the ground and took Sadie's empty plate. "In fact, I'd like to take Gidget back to the stable. Be right back."

"I'll go with you. It'll feel good to walk off some of this food."

With a whistle for Fly and a stop at the trash bin to throw out their disposable plates, Mick found Gidget with Beatie, Thatcher and Wyatt on the cabin's porch. "Hey there. I'm here to steal Gidget and put her to bed."

"Aw. That time already?" Beatie laid her cheek atop Gidget's head. "Enjoy your beauty sleep, sweet girl. I love you."

When Gidget nuzzled Beatie's side, Sadie grinned. "Looks like the feeling is mutual, Beatie."

"I'm sure she loves everyone," Beatie insisted before kissing the mini horse on the nose. "This critter has the biggest heart I've ever seen."

Wyatt glanced at his watch. "Speaking of bedtime, Luna and Rose should be asleep about now. I feel strange not being there to put them down, but Mom and Dad are babysitting."

Beatie gave Gidget one last, lingering pat. "They sure enjoy being grandparents, don't they?"

"You can say that again. They love and adore those girls."

Mick did, too, but he couldn't help wishing his aunt and uncle had also been able to muster up some love for him. Or at least could have told him they felt that way, even if it was a lie. Because *love* was a strong word, with the power to heal a person.

Or break him.

Mick did what he always did when the old wound nagged at him. He prayed and then reminded himself of his blessings. Even if some of them felt hollow. "Come on, Gidget."

"Is everything okay?" Sadie nudged his arm with hers as they walked to the stable. "Are you thinking about that dog at the clinic?"

He thought he had hidden his emotions better than that.

Then again, Sadie was perceptive. "There's a tech there, and he'll text me if he needs me. Let's get Gidget settled so we can get back to the party."

She sighed. "You can say a lot of things about my dad, but he knew how to throw a good Christmas party. That's why we model our parties now on what we remember from the alternating Christmases we spent here as kids."

"Fun memories?" He opened the stable door.

"Sure."

"That didn't sound convincing." He got to work settling in Gidget for the night. There wasn't much to do, especially since Wyatt would be here later for the nighttime routine with Gidget and the mares. "Did your parents fight more during the holidays?"

"Yes, but—never mind. We're supposed to be in party mode, not a therapy session."

"Hey, we're safe for each other to vent to, right? You listened to me complain about the clinic."

"Leonard not ordering equipment is a valid complaint."

"All feelings are valid." Despite the way his family avoided acknowledging the negative ones. "Tell me."

She hesitated, then puffed out a breath. "I think our parents spent so much time loathing each other that they had very little energy left over for us kids, if that makes sense. And when they did pay attention to us, they didn't go deep. Talking about us to others, they would state the obvious. How smart Natalie was. How Dove could whip up a fabulous cake at age ten. Thatcher wasn't even their kid, but dad talked about how great he was at the ranch."

Mick's stomach sank. "What did they say about you?"

"That I was quiet. Even though I tried every way I could to get them to notice me, but no matter what I did or how unquiet I tried to be, I felt like they never noticed. When it came to my career, they would tell people that I found a summer job in Goldenrod and never left it. It hurt that they never realized I chose this career because I liked it. I was good at it. I tried to explain it to my parents once, but they didn't understand. Or maybe didn't care. I don't doubt my parents' love for me, but it always felt like they didn't know the real me."

"I'm sorry, Sadie. Because the real you is amazing." Mick shut the latch behind him and faced Sadie in the center aisle. She was such a wonderful person. How could anyone overlook her? But the pain in her dark eyes was palpable. "Your sisters know you, though."

"Yes, but they make assumptions about me. I don't always feel understood. Maybe it's my fault for not being clearer, but it's not easy to talk about." She gave him a watery smile. "It's easier to talk to you."

"I feel the same. Makes me wonder if it's worse to be loved but not known or known but not loved?"

Her mouth formed an O. "Do you mean those two girlfriends you had? Because they didn't deserve you."

"Thanks, but I don't think—sorry, we're supposed to be talking about you."

"I'm done. Now, tell me what you meant."

He led her out of the stable into the cool, dark night. "Well, Gary and Jillian know me well. I lived with them the majority of my childhood, and they could tell how much I wanted to work with Grandpa Hank at the vet clinic. They care about me and want me in their lives, but they don't love me."

Sadie stopped walking. "That can't be true."

"They've never once said it."

Her brow furrowed. "Is that their way? To rarely speak the *L* word?"

"They don't often say it, but they did to Wyatt. That was hard for me as a kid." Still hard, to be honest. "I used to tell them I loved them, but eventually I stopped."

Her mouth and eyes were round as quarters. "Oh, Mick. You deserved so much better than that. I can't believe you told them you loved them and…and nothing."

"I wasn't a member of their family. Aunt Jillian told Wyatt straight up, and I overheard. I also picked up on other things that communicated I wasn't Jillian and Gary's son, by blood or her heart. And it might not feel good, but there's something to be said for knowing where you stand with people. So, when she got persnickety on Thanksgiving about Rose and Luna not calling me Uncle Mick? That is her way of reminding me."

"That's…awful. How can you say all that with such an even tone?" Sadie's voice shook. "That has to hurt."

"Thankfully, my sense of worth isn't rooted in my family. God's love is unconditional."

"That's what first drew me to God too. I realized He *knew* me—good things and bad—but He loved me anyway."

"To be known and loved—we humans want it, don't we?"

"We need it." Sadie's sad eyes hardened. "I'm so angry. I want to have a good long talk with Jillian."

Nice as it felt to have her want to defend him, it wouldn't do any good. "Thanks, but they aren't open about problems the way you Daltons are. In fact, the Teagues avoid difficult discussions at all costs. And I'm okay, Sadie. Honest. Now you know me better, though. And I know you. And it does feel good to be known, doesn't it?"

Her eyes softened like she might cry. "I hurt for you."

"And I hurt for you."

So he did the only thing he could do. The only thing he really wanted to do. He opened his arms and pulled her close to comfort her. Just like she comforted him the day she asked him to go to Blair's wedding.

Her head tucked under his chin, and she snuggled against his coat, wrapping her arms around his waist. She smelled of woodsmoke, and he wanted to breathe it in for a long while. Not thinking about their families or past hurts or whether or not he could hug her like this once they weren't fake dating anymore.

Just existing.

"Um, excuse me." Natalie's voice broke them apart. "I came to tell you it's time for s'mores."

"You didn't mention s'mores." Mick tried to lighten the mood. "Maybe I should go back to the stable."

"No escaping." Sadie met his smile with one of her own. "Take a seat. I'll be right back."

She skipped into the cabin, and when she returned and met him at the firepit, she held a plastic baggie. "I couldn't have you missing out on the fun, so I prepared a marshmallow replacement for you."

"Are those bananas? Thanks, Sadie. This is going to taste good."

He skewered the thin banana slices to warm them. Then, when they took on a deeper shade of gold in the firelight, he sandwiched them and a square of milk chocolate between two graham crackers. The bananas didn't melt into a gooey glue to hold the s'more together, of course, but they made a tasty substitute.

The pull of someone's gaze drew his attention. Natalie and Wyatt watched him. Not with hostility, but as if he were a puzzle they couldn't crack.

No one understood him like Sadie, though. And apparently, she didn't feel understood by most of the world either.

"What are you thinking about so seriously?"

"What do you mean?"

"You have a crease right here." Her forefinger tapped the space between his eyes.

"I was thinking that I know you, Sadie Dalton. Enough to suspect you'd like another s'more."

Her laugh was as sweet as Christmas bells. "I would—oh, Mick." Her hand went to his sleeve. "Snow."

Sure enough, there was a flake on his jacket. Then another joined it.

"Now, that is what I call the perfect ending to a Foxtail Farm–staff Christmas party."

"And our fourth date of Christmas." Except even as he said it, his gaze landed on her lips. Their kiss at Blair's wedding was…not what he should be thinking about. But if he kissed her now, her lips would probably taste like graham crackers.

And marshmallows. But even that unpleasant fact wasn't enough to keep him from wanting to kiss her anyway.

They had been vulnerable tonight, and that sense of closeness surely accounted for part of the pull he felt toward her. But they were best friends. He couldn't jeopardize their relationship.

So rather than kiss her, he stuffed his s'more in his mouth.

Chapter Eight

The next morning, Sadie's phone alarm tugged her out of a dream and into the dark, cold reality of predawn.

She groaned, but there was no hitting the snooze button. Saturdays were busy at the farmstand. She slipped out from the flannel sheets, shoved her feet into her fuzzy slippers and trudged to the window to open the blinds. Had those snowflakes from last night turned into something more?

They had! The world was blanketed in white. Well, gray in the thin glow of the landscape lighting. It was only an inch or two deep, but farther up the mountain, there would be more. The youth group kids were going to have a blast at the sledding party today.

First things first.

She dressed in snowpants and a Fair Isle–style red sweater embellished with reindeer and snowflakes. After donning her coat and accessories, she walked to the farmstand, following tracks in the snow that were Dove's shoe size. She let herself into the bakery, and the aromas of bread and pastries made her stomach rumble. "Morning, Dove."

"Morning." Her younger sister, clad in jeans, a black turtleneck and a white baker's coat, rolled out pie dough. "Did you have fun last night?"

"I always love the staff party. Great work, as always."

"Thanks, and you too—but I meant *with Mick*. For fake dating, you two sure looked cozy."

"If you mean huddled together for warmth at the firepit, then yes. It was freezing." Sadie did not want to talk about looking cozy with Mick, so she grasped on to the topic of the weather. "Wasn't it wonderful that it started to snow last night?"

"It was the perfect ending to the evening."

Sadie poured herself a mug of coffee and snagged a day-old cheese Danish for her breakfast. "We got the perfect amount overnight too. Not enough to block the roads, so we should expect a surge of visitors who will drop by and buy your pies when they come up the mountain to play in the snow."

"You get to play in the snow today, yourself."

"Yep. Elena is covering me at the farmstand."

"I think Wyatt and Natalie are chaperones too. You can double date."

"Not much of a date when you're hanging with the youth group." But she still counted it as their fifth date because they'd been asked to do this together.

Sadie slipped back into the cold and unlocked the door to her workshop. She flipped on the fluorescent bulbs overhead as well as the heater and the sound system, which was set to a holiday-music station.

She filled her watering can and carried it into the farmstand, where she tended the poinsettias and the rosemary bushes shaped like Christmas trees, inhaling their savory aroma. Then she returned to the workshop and logged on the computer so she could go over holiday inventory. By the time the farmstand was open, she had also completed two romantic bouquets for the farmstand's stock—red roses mingled with salal, eucalyptus and golden fir.

When a knock came at the back door, she wiped her hands on her apron. "Come on in, Mick."

Mick slipped in, looking like a lumberjack with his brawny build clad in a blue plaid flannel shirt, heavy boots and a fawn jacket. Stubble lined his square jaw, and his brown, wavy locks were mussed, as if he'd been outdoors for hours already today. "How did you know it would be me? I'm early."

"No one else knocks." Her sisters, Thatcher and Elena always strode right in. "No Fly today? I thought you'd bring her."

"She loves the snow, but since it's a long day today and our focus has to be on the kids, I thought it might be better to leave her at home. We've already had a good long fetch session, and I promised her we'd play some more later." He leaned against the worktable. "Are you about ready to go?"

"One second while I tell Elena goodbye and grab my purse."

A minute later, they were in his truck, and they arrived at the community park at about the same time as the other chaperones, fifteen minutes before the kids were scheduled to arrive. After carrying supplies to the area they'd reserved at the crest of the slope, they joined in prayer for a fun, safe time for the church's middle and high schoolers. Then they got busy unpacking sleds, plastic discs, toboggans and inner tubes from car trunks; brushing snow off picnic tables; and starting charcoal fires in two of the park's barbecues to grill hot dogs. Sadie had just finished spreading blankets over the picnic benches with Natalie when the first carload of kids arrived.

"Here we go," Natalie said.

Sadie greeted the ones she knew and met the friends they'd invited, but when Kelsey stepped out of her mom's

SUV, she welcomed her with a hug. Even though Kelsey was participating in the living nativity, Sadie hadn't had much opportunity to chat with her since Blair's wedding. She had no idea if the girl was still struggling with her self-image, but she was determined to assure Kelsey with words and actions that she cared for her. "Good to see you, Kels."

Kelsey's wide grin held no sense of self-consciousness over her braces. "Are you going to sled, Sadie?"

"At some point."

"Then come with me now. I'm too chicken to go alone." Kelsey pulled Sadie by the arm toward the kids lined up at the edge of the snowy slope.

Laughing, Sadie complied, and within seconds it was their turn. She sat behind Kelsey atop a banana-yellow toboggan.

"Do you two want a push?"

Sadie knew the voice behind her as well as she knew her own reflection. She turned and glared at Mick's smirking face. "Don't you dare, Mick David Larson."

"Do it!" Kelsey yelled at the same time.

"Can't say no to Kelsey." His words were soft, but the pressure of Mick's hands against Sadie's back wasn't.

Kelsey screamed in delight as they zipped downhill in a thrilling rush. Sadie shrieked and laughed in turns before they sputtered to a stop at the bottom.

"I want to do that again!" Kelsey was off the toboggan in a flash, ready to hike back up the hill.

"That was fun." Sadie helped her carry the toboggan back up the hill, where they relinquished it to a red-haired girl waiting for a turn. The girl smiled shyly at Kelsey. "Want to go with me?"

"Sure, Vivienne. Do you want to be in the front or back?"

Glad to see the kids interacting, Sadie made a beeline for Mick, who sent some boys flying down the slope in an inner tube. "Hey, Mick, can you help me find something? I lost it right here, at the top of the slope."

"Sure. An earring?" His brow furrowed as he stared at the ground. "A glove?"

"My stomach. It didn't go with the rest of me down the hill."

He laughed. "I didn't push you that hard."

"No, but if I were you, I'd watch your back."

"I'd rather watch yours while we take a turn with the sled." His smile turned sly. "This is a date, you know. It'd be weird if we didn't go down together."

Why not? Wyatt and Natalie were on their way down right now, and Pastor Luke was on his way back up the slope with an inner tube in hand. "Let's get in line."

They didn't have long to wait, and within minutes, Mick straddled an antique-looking sled. Gingerly, she sat in front of him and tucked in her knees. He wrapped his arms around her, shifted his legs and closed the gap between them. "Hold tight," he whispered in her ear.

"You, too, or I'm toast. Whoa!"

She had no idea who pushed them, but they sped downhill so fast they went airborne over a small bump. He laughed in her ear, and she started laughing, too. Her ribs hurt from it when they reached the bottom.

She gasped for air as she hopped off the sled. "What was that?"

"I don't know, but it was awesome." He scooped up the sled.

Her hands pressed her aching rib cage. "I don't know why I can't stop laughing."

"Because you're happy."

"Or delirious from fear," she joked, adjusting her knit cap back over her ears.

Then they were surrounded by kids, and their roles as

chaperones took precedence over their wild ride down the hill. Sadie split from Mick to chat with a group of girls while he met Wyatt at the grill.

Pretty soon, the aroma of grilled hot dogs filled the air. "Ten minutes till we eat," Wyatt announced.

"That's plenty of time to play a game of snowball toss." Kelsey pointed at one of the picnic tables, where someone had set up two pyramids fashioned out of six upturned plastic cups each.

"Go for it." Natalie popped open a bottle of ketchup. "I'll watch."

"You should play," Kelsey said. "You and Sadie. Sister versus sister."

How could they say no to that? Sadie smiled. "You first, Nat."

"Let's do this." Natalie moved to the right side of the table and scooped a handful of snow off the ground. "Here goes." She tossed the ball, and it knocked the uppermost cup off in a splatter of snow.

After cheering for her sister, Sadie packed snow into a ball. Then she wound her arm, threw it and missed by at least six inches.

She gave a good-natured groan while the girls laughed.

Natalie's next throw knocked out four cups. Sadie's toss went farther afield than the first. Well, this was embarrassing, but it was all good fun.

Natalie's third attempt knocked one more cup to the ground. She came over to pat Sadie's shoulder. "Pack your snow harder."

It was packed plenty hard.

"Aim a little to the left," Kelsey said.

"And use more force when you throw," another girl instructed.

She put her all into it. Aimed farther left.

It flew way too far, way too left, smacking Mick on the back of the head.

Her hand went to her mouth as Mick spun around, spluttering.

"Uh-oh." Kelsey giggled.

Mick gaped at Sadie. "That was you?"

"It was an accident. Honest."

"Uh-huh."

"It was. Ask the girls. I have lousy aim."

"That's true," one whispered loudly.

"Are you asking for a snowball fight?" Mick's brow arched as he bent to swipe snow from the ground.

"No way. The hot dogs are almost ready and I do not— Mick, you stay away from me, Mick!"

He ran for her, dashed behind her, and dropped a handful of snow beneath her scarf at the back of her neck. Down it went, spreading over her back. She hopped away, shaking out her sweater. "Mick David Larson!"

"That's the second time today you used my middle name." He scooped up another handful of snow.

"No, no, please." She held up her hands. "Icy cold gives me migraines sometimes, remember?"

His hand fell. So did his smile.

A ball of snow splattered against his chest, but it wasn't from Sadie's hand. Some of the boys seemed to think this was the start of a snow war, and within seconds, the park had erupted in flying snow, whoops and squeals of delight.

Not Sadie, though. Hoping to avoid another migraine, she hurried off to the picnic tables.

"Sadie, I'm so sorry." Mick followed her, his forehead as furrowed as a plowed field. "Even though we literally went through your migraine triggers a few days ago, I wasn't thinking. Honestly. I thought you were inviting a playful snowball fight."

His apology touched her, but how could he think that? "I'm not sure how you got that impression. I told you I hit you by accident."

"I thought you were teasing. I mean, we've been joshing each other all day. You used my middle name, then I pushed you down the slope, and we were laughing so hard." He peered down at her. "Are you okay? Do you have a headache? I feel so bad."

"I'm fine. And now that you put it that way, it makes sense why you thought I was teasing."

"I promise never to do it again."

He looked so sorrowful that any lingering annoyance at her cold back melted. "Thank you. I wish I could promise my aim will improve, but since I can't do that, I'll try my hardest never to hit you with an errant snowball again."

He didn't smile. "I'm so upset at myself for forgetting how ice affects you."

"I've got migraine medicine in my purse if I need it, and right now I'm okay. I shouldn't have barked at you."

"I deserved it. I would never want to hurt you on purpose, Sadie."

"I know, Mick."

His lips twitched. "Is this our first fight?"

"I can't remember. It's our first since we started *dating*, though." She made air quotes.

"Should we act like dating people, then?"

Her stomach did a somersault. "Wha—what?"

"Hug it out." His icy blue eyes sparkled with mirth. "Did you think I was going to say kiss and make up?"

"Pfft." Yes, but she'd never admit it.

She might have said yes, too, if they weren't at a youth

group function, but she had to put a stop to those dangerous types of thoughts—now, before she regretted the most important aspect of their December dating arrangement.

Its looming expiration date.

Dropping snow down her back? What a stupid, juvenile thing to do.

Mick mentally kicked himself all the way back to the grill. Hopefully, his side hug conveyed his relief that Sadie had forgiven him for shoving snow down her neck.

"What do you think you're doing?" Wyatt was in his face before Mick reached the grill, and he was almost growling.

"Coming to help you cook hot dogs—I'm kidding. I know you're talking about Sadie." He held up his hands. "I was irresponsible, okay? I forgot cold could trigger one of her migraines."

"You were irresponsible, all right, but I'm talking about the flirting."

"We don't…flirt." The word tasted weird in his mouth.

Wyatt muttered something unintelligible.

"We tease. Always have, always will."

Wyatt barked out a laugh. "Snow on her neck? That's flirting."

"I pelted your neck with snow all the time when we were kids."

Wyatt wasn't fazed. "Have you kissed her?"

"At the wedding." Everyone knew that. "And it only lasted, like, a few seconds."

"If you were kissing someone you didn't want to kiss, it wouldn't last a hundredth of that amount of time, even for show." Wyatt's thick eyebrows scrunched up. "Is this relationship still fake?"

"It is."

"Then you need to act like it. All the time. I don't want Sadie getting hurt because you led her on."

This was coming from a place of concern, but it was starting to upset Mick. "She won't get the wrong idea. She knows where we stand."

"Where you *stood*, maybe, but things are different between you two now. Everyone can see it. Thatcher might think your fake relationship is funny, and Natalie and Dove think it's weirdly good for Sadie for some reason, but I'm not happy about it." Wyatt's expression softened a fraction. "You're my cousin, but she's my sister-in-law, man. Be careful with her. No more kissing."

"I hadn't planned on kissing her the first time."

"Just make sure there's not a second one, Mick."

Wyatt was making too much of this. Mick and Sadie were fine. That was all that mattered.

But Mick went out of his way to be the perfect gentleman for the rest of the day.

And the next day, too, when they attended the church's Christmas pageant together and the younger kids told the story of Jesus's birth in a much simpler but no less beautiful way than the living nativity would do.

Mick and Sadie's date the following evening, the cookie exchange at Blair's, was pleasant and light, with no deep conversation or touching of any kind. But Tuesday night, Mick took Sadie's hand to steady her on the slick, damp street outside the diner where they'd finally eaten BLTs before leaving to sing carols with Sadie's Bible study group at the nursing home.

He intended to maintain the attentive but platonic pattern tonight for their ninth date, his aunt and uncle's annual holiday party. Their place, Manzanita Ranch, was named after native trees that bore tiny apple-like fruit in the summer, and it was more than the home where Mick grew up. It was his uncle's livelihood, where he bred quarter horses and stabled horses for clients. Tonight's appetizer bash was Gary and Jillian's way of thanking their business acquaintances.

Sadie and her family had long attended these parties since the Teagues and Daltons had been connected through Wyatt and Natalie for years. But this was the first time Sadie had arrived with Mick instead of her family.

It was also the first time Mick had paid attention to what she wore to the party. The cream-colored sweater dress flattered her lean figure, and he liked how her blond hair fell in soft waves against her shoulders.

She caught him looking. "Are you thinking what I'm thinking?"

That she was prettier than a Christmas rose? "Probably not. What are you thinking?"

"I'm wondering if it would be tacky to take more than one of those little cups of shrimp cocktail making the rounds."

"Nope. Not tacky. And that wasn't crossing my mind at all."

Her gaze followed a server carrying the tray of pink-tailed shrimp. "You're thinking about the nativity, aren't you?"

Now that she mentioned it, he probably *should* be thinking about it. "It's only three days away."

"But everything's under control. Robin doesn't need us at the final rehearsals tonight or tomorrow. Everything else is in great shape: the sets, the costumes, the animals. Even the weather forecast." She stood on tiptoe to speak into his ear. "Maybe you'd rather be at rehearsal because this is our seventh night out in a row and you're tired of parties."

Or maybe he just didn't feel entirely comfortable at this one.

Even though he'd grown up here, lately he'd been thinking more and more about his childhood. Although he was grateful to Aunt Jillian and Uncle Gary for taking him in and supporting him, and although he'd come to terms with their inability to love him a long time ago, knowing where he stood was less satisfying than it once had been.

Why was he thinking about this now? This was a party. "Let's chase that guy with the shrimp."

"Now you're talking."

Over the next hour, they nibbled shrimp, chatted with Sadie's sisters, Wyatt and Thatcher, sipped more punch, and mingled with Manzanita Ranch's clients. But there were definitely some people missing, and when he and Sadie stepped up to the punch table, he finally had the opportunity to ask her if she'd seen Beatie and Dutch.

"No, and I haven't heard a word from him about her medical tests. Granted, I haven't been in the orchard lately, but when I do see them out and about, he's protective of her. She's always on his arm." She bit her lip. "Do you have any idea what could be wrong?"

"I'm not sure, but I'm praying it's nothing major." He might have said more, but Aunt Jillian, shimmering in silver sequins that matched the decor, floated toward them.

Lord, have I truly forgiven Jillian for not loving me—something she can't even help? Please show me how to get over the hurt I thought I'd conquered. Show me how to love her and Uncle Gary more and more because You love them. Not because I want them to love me back.

"Great party, Aunt Jillian." He prayed as he hugged her.

Sadie gave his aunt a brief side hug too. "Jillian, you are so talented. Every time I attend a party in this barn it's better than the last. I love the silver color scheme."

"Well, my trick is to use the same basic decorations every year, but I always change out the colors for a fresh look."

Other than the ten-foot Douglas fir in the corner, the greenery was artificial, from the pine swags to the mistletoe dangling over the threshold—Mick had been sure to spy that out in advance.

The floral arrangement on the punch table wasn't fake, though. The toy sleigh was full of real red and white flowers. It wasn't silver and white, like the rest of his aunt's decor tonight, but it was well done. "Did you make that, Sadie?"

She shook her head. "It's a popular offering from Goldenrod Floral Design. I crafted dozens of these when I worked there."

"Some clients sent it tonight, along with their last-minute regrets that they couldn't attend." Aunt Jillian adjusted the red sleigh on the table. "It's sweet, but unfortunately, I can't take it back to the house with me. The cats will either nibble it or bat it off the counter. Why don't you take it home with you at the end of the evening, Sadie?" Aunt Jillian's serene smile suddenly disappeared. "Oh, how thoughtless of me. You're a florist."

"Actually, if you can't find someone else to take them, I'd be happy to."

"But you have oodles of blooms at your disposal. Surely you don't intend to…sell the arrangement at the farmstand?" Aunt Jillian's tone dripped with disapproval.

Mick couldn't believe his ears. He'd just been praying to better love his aunt, but now he was mortified on Sadie's behalf. "Sadie would never pass off someone else's work as her own, Aunt Jillian, much less profit off it."

"Not to mention it would cause all sorts of problems for our bookkeeper, Bliss." Sadie, bless her, laughed off his aunt's uncharitable question. "No, I would drop it off at the nursing home on Ponderosa Street tomorrow. One of the residents would surely appreciate it."

"Oh." Aunt Jillian's face reddened. "What a lovely thought. Let's plan on you taking it, then, Sadie. Oh, there's

Gary, waving me over to talk to someone. Have a good time, dears. Try the stuffed artichokes."

The moment she was gone, Mick reached for Sadie's hands. "I am so sorry, Sadie. She jumped to a ridiculous conclusion, and I hate that she didn't apologize. I don't think she realized—but it doesn't matter. I'll talk to her." Even though it wouldn't do any good.

His aunt would change the subject, like she always did when he broached something confrontational or unpleasant. But this wasn't about him. It was about Sadie, and he wouldn't let her be disparaged in any way. His blood boiled at the thought of Sadie being insulted or hurt.

"Please don't say anything." Sadie squeezed his hands. "I'm sure she's overwhelmed by everything on her to-do list. Christmas on its own is a lot, but she's been working on this party, plus the nativity sets. You and I can relate to having too much to do and not enough time to do it in."

"You're far kinder than I am."

"No, but at this time of year, a lot of situations call for EGR."

"I've known you forever, but I have no idea what EGR is."

"Extra Grace Required."

"That's what it means?" He filled her cup with punch. "So that's why you forgave me for the snow incident."

"Maybe." Her smile was sly.

He tipped his head at a server walking past with a shrimp tray. "Want to grab half a dozen more shrimp and head out?"

"Yes." Her smile proved she didn't take him seriously. "But it would be rude. Come on, we can get through this. We only have three more nights in a row of events, and then we get a break until Christmas Eve."

"Our twelfth date," he reminded her. "We're going to church together after the party, right? And then I thought we could take the long way home and look at Christmas lights."

"Yes. A hundred times, yes."

"Whatcha saying yes to, honey?"

So there was Beatie at last, decked out in a red turtleneck and a vest striped like a candy cane. She clung to Dutch's arm and grinned at Mick and Sadie. "We just got here, and my, oh my, what did we walk into? A marriage proposal?"

A *what?* Mick's breath whooshed out of him like he'd been kicked in the gut by an ornery mule. Meanwhile, his brain screamed a chorus of *no*s.

Sadie responded by laughing. "Very funny, Beatie. You know very well Mick would never propose at a punch bowl."

"I suppose it's not romantic." Beatie chuckled. "But you two have been together, friends or otherwise, for years now. Time's ticking."

"All right, darlin', they got the hint. Let's greet our hosts. Have fun, you two." Dutch tucked Beatie's hand higher on the arm of his blue snowflake-patterned sweater and led her into the crowd.

Mick found his breath again. "Yikes."

"Tell me about it." Sadie drained her punch. "I'm…a little sensitive about people talking like that. Like love and marriage are the be all and end all in life. Or that I didn't want them in the first place."

Wait, she wanted to get married? Now? Or was this past tense?

Why was this a surprise? She probably would have married Easton Morris if he hadn't dumped her.

Mick didn't like how the idea made him feel, but ultimately, it wasn't his business. "It rubs me wrong, too, but let's shake off their well-intentioned nagging."

"Nagging from matchmakers whom we love so much that we're *fake dating*." She mouthed the last two words.

Thatcher strode toward the punch bowl, clamping a plate

of stuffed artichokes in his large hands. "Hey, you two. Two things. First, have you tried these? They're fantastic."

"They are," Mick agreed.

"Second, you gotta be more careful where you choose to stand." Thatcher glanced up.

Mick copied him.

Great. More mistletoe.

"This evening keeps getting better and better." Sadie sighed. "I spotted the sprig over the door, but I missed this one. Let's move somewhere mistletoe-free."

"No way." Thatcher cackled. "Dutch and Beatie just sent me over to tell you to 'obey the mistletoe rules.' So here I am, to ensure you do."

Mick was glad his back was to Dutch and Beatie so they couldn't hear his next words. "Dude, you know we're not really dating."

"So?"

"You delivered your message. You don't have to enforce it."

"But it's funny." Grinning, Thatcher stuffed an artichoke heart in his mouth.

Wyatt had said something like that, how Thatcher thought this was hilarious but Wyatt disapproved. Feeling like a cad, Mick took Sadie's elbow and led her away from the punch bowl. "We did the mistletoe thing once. I won't put you through that again."

"It wasn't exactly torture. For me, anyway."

"Me neither." He didn't want her to think kissing her was unpleasant. But he didn't want to tell her that it was far nicer than he had expected either.

So nice that he wouldn't mind doing it again.

But kissing her was trouble with a capital *T*. "Sadie," he began.

"It's okay."

He wasn't sure if she was saying it was fine if they did kiss or fine if they didn't, but before he could ask, his phone buzzed in his pocket.

"Saved by the bell." It felt like he was about to break into a sweat.

"I'm getting something too." She dug into her purse. "It's a group text from Robin. They're still at rehearsal but…oh no."

Mick saw it too. One of the nativity sets had fallen over. He read ahead quickly, praying all the while.

He let out a relieved breath. "Thankfully, no one was hurt."

"But I think we'd better go." She tapped a reply on her phone. "I'm telling Robin we'll be there in a few minutes."

"I'll make our regrets to Aunt Jillian and Uncle Gary while you tell your sisters. Meet you at the door—but not under the mistletoe."

Thankfully, his attempt at a joke didn't fall flat. Her lips twitched as she glanced up at him. "I'll be standing about three miles away from it."

The prospect of a wrecked nativity set did a decent job kicking thoughts of kissing Sadie out of his head. He finally had to admit to himself that he was attracted to Sadie, but he reminded himself that attraction always faded sooner or later.

He and Sadie would be back to their old mistletoe-less friendship by New Year's Eve.

There was no cause for concern there.

Unlike the living nativity. Mick tugged his truck keys from his pocket.

Chapter Nine

Thursday afternoon, Sadie yawned long and loud in the workroom. Twice.

Last night, she and Mick had rushed from the party at Manzanita Ranch, unsure how big of a disaster the set collapse would be. Thankfully, the single wall and the attached straw "roof" that had fallen were not part of a set where actors would be, so they hadn't been anchored as securely as they should have been.

Today, Jillian and a few members of her crew had shored up the weak area and stabilized the rest of the walls so it wouldn't be a problem on Saturday.

The minute the set was secure, however, Dove had let out a frustrated wail that could be heard all the way to the parking lot. The commercial oven had gone cold. With dozens of pies to make before the nativity in two days, this was a huge problem. A repair person would arrive tomorrow, but in the meantime, Dove had pies in the tiny ovens at all four farmhouse apartments, as well as the oven at Natalie's house.

Sadie had been running back and forth to take pies in and out of the oven in her apartment, but she still had her own job to do. This floral arrangement for a new baby was supposed to be picked up in half an hour. Pink and white spray roses, pink gerbera daisies—

"There you are, Sadie."

Sadie looked up at the farmstand door to find Dutch and Beatie, their expressions as distraught as kids who'd just found out Christmas was canceled.

"What's happened?" *Lord, is it Beatie's test results?* A skitter of fear rushed through her.

"Paula's been trying to get ahold of you. Phil, our Joseph in the nativity?" Beatie shook her head. "His appendix just exploded."

"Ruptured," Dutch clarified.

"That's what I said." Beatie spread out her fingers like fireworks going off.

Appendixes didn't—oh, it didn't matter. "Poor Phil. Is he okay? That can be dangerous."

"He'll be fine, according to Paula. But they have to stay at the hospital in La Mesa. She's sorry about missing the nativity and leaving you up the creek."

"No, she's exactly where she needs to be, and the nativity should be the last thing on their minds." But two thirds of the Holy Family were out now, and considering the other third was a plastic-headed doll?

Sadie scooped up her phone, right where she'd left it on her table. Sure enough, the screen revealed several missed texts and calls. With all the running back and forth, she hadn't checked it in a while. Her temples started to throb. *Not another migraine, please.*

Dutch adjusted his large-lensed eyeglasses. "What are you going to do?"

"I don't know," she answered honestly. "Pray, for starters."

"We'll join you," Beatie said. "But I think you'd better pray while you work, because the poinsettias are a hazard."

"What about them?" The display at the farmstand's entrance looked fine, if sparse, since her shipment hadn't arrived yet. "Did they fall over?"

Beatie shook her head. "No, they're all upright. Pretty, too, but meddlesome. I doubt you'll sell that truckload before Christmas."

"Truckload?" Sadie's stomach swooshed. "Excuse me."

She dashed through the farmstand, past the shelves of apple geegaws and candles, bins of fruit and vegetables, the display of red, pink and white poinsettias and all the way outside, where Elena watched as a delivery truck pulled out of the lot—one Sadie recognized as belonging to a floral distributor she worked with. And all around her on the ground were poinsettias in varieties she remembered from the website last week.

Ice Punch, Sonora White Glitter, Marco Polo, White Rose Marble, Lemon Glow, Orange Spice and Jingle Bell Rock. Bracts of red, white, pink, coral, gold and orange. Speckled, striped, variegated. She had never seen so many poinsettia plants.

"What is this?" She shimmied through the plants to reach Elena. "Did they give us the wrong order?" And who in Goldenrod needed what looked like a few hundred of these?

"I don't think so." Elena cringed. "It says Foxtail Farm on the paperwork."

Sadie took the paper. The recipient listed Foxtail, all right, but Sadie had not ordered five hundred plants. Regardless of whether this was a clerical error or an act of incompetence, these plants had to go back. "I'm going to pull up my confirmation email to verify things on my end and then call the distributor."

"In the meantime, what should I do with these? We can't just leave them here."

True. They blocked the entrance and exit, a fire hazard as

well as a deterrent to shoppers. "Let's clear a path by shoving them to either side of the entrance and displays. I'll help once I have a hand free."

She scrolled through the emails on her phone to find her confirmation email from the distributor, then realized she had never opened it. But surely she hadn't—

Mercy, she had.

Five. Hundred. Poinsettias.

How?

She thought back. The night she'd ordered them, she'd had a migraine. She'd ordered gauze and then looked at these varieties before bed. She'd been dreaming of a candy-colored Christmas with poinsettias lining the farmstand and paths, and she'd added them to the cart, but she had definitely saved them for later. Which had turned out to be a wise choice, because she had already forgotten that gingerbread-candy idea, and she was glad to have been reminded of it now.

But not like this. She'd wanted sixteen plants. Not five hundred—

Oh. Fly had stepped on her laptop, hadn't she?

Sadie thought the screen had refreshed, but what if Fly had hit a button that sent the computer back to the previous screen before Sadie moved these items out of her cart?

She should have checked. This was all her fault.

And now she had to fix it. The plants were beautiful, fresh and bright, but Foxtail couldn't afford to keep them. It was too late to execute a candy-colored Christmas now. Besides, not even a quarter of these would sell, with less than a week until Christmas.

Hopefully, the distributor would take them back. She might have to pay a fee, but what else could she do? She tapped their phone number on the screen, and with her free hand she helped Elena clear a path while she waited to speak to a customer service representative, kicking herself all the while for causing such a mess.

The nativity was in two days, and there was hardly space to walk around the farmstand. Poinsettias in abundance, but no Joseph, no Mary and no fully functional bakery. Meanwhile, the holiday tune playing over the sound system was "Joy to the World," a striking counterpoint to the misery swirling in her stomach.

More like *Stress to the world*. Now she understood how people turned into grinches this time of year.

But then the lyrics hit her.

Joy.

A solid reminder of what Christmas was all about.

Joy to the world! The Lord is come. Let earth receive her king. Let every heart prepare Him room, and heaven and nature sing...

Joy as a response to a gift that wouldn't fade like flowers. God's love lasted forever.

Five hundred unwanted potted plants couldn't break that sort of joy.

Repentant, she shut her eyes. *Lord, help me refocus on You. On what this holiday is all about, not just two thousand years ago in Bethlehem, but on all the ways You continue to show love to a weary world.*

She finished praying. Moved more plants. Untwisted a bent plastic trim tag on a pink-and-white poinsettia.

Her fingers froze on the tag as her imagination sparked.

Could she? Her idea was risky. She should call Mick first to get his approval, but he had texted that he'd been called out to a ranch out of cell range to help one of the livestock vets he knew, and had asked if they could meet at the shelter party tonight instead of riding together. She couldn't wait until tonight to decide.

It might not pan out, but why not try?

She hung up on the instrumental hold music playing over the phone. "Change of plans, Elena."

Elena's black, curly hair flopped over her eyes as she looked up from dragging pots of bright yellow poinsettias. "Do you want them somewhere else?"

"I do." Sadie took a deep breath. "Give me five minutes to grab the cart."

Later that evening, Mick let himself into the Victorian-era home of Odette Lamott, the hostess of tonight's animal shelter "paw-ty," which he couldn't say with a straight face. He whistled at the beauty of the restored home, decorated to the hilt for the holidays. It was a gorgeous setting for the shelter's staff, volunteers and donors to eat, mingle and enjoy. Making his way through the clusters of guests in the front of the house, he had his eyes peeled for two women.

The first was easier to find: Odette herself. He thanked the fifty-something woman with short, gray hair, then spied Wyatt and Natalie, who graciously pointed out Sadie across the room and looking pretty in a dress the shade of a blue spruce. Smiling his thanks, Mick made a beeline for her, refusing to think about how seeing her felt like coming home.

"You made it." Sadie set down her plate of cheese and crackers to give him a brief one-armed hug.

"Sorry I'm late. What a day." He had been out of cell range this afternoon, and once he was closer to a cell tower, his phone had pinged with so many alerts he'd grown concerned and pulled over to look at them.

They'd all been about poor Phil and his appendix, except for the last, from Leonard, asking if Mick could return to the clinic to treat a cat with a respiratory infection so Leonard could go to a doctor's appointment.

Mick had texted Sadie that he would be even later than he'd expected, especially since he still had to run home to tend to Fly and change clothes.

"I feel awful about Phil." Sadie shook her head.

"Me too. Paula was so apologetic about us having to find replacements for them, but I'm more concerned about Phil. God will provide a new Mary and Joseph for the nativity." He selected a small plate.

"I didn't see the texts for a while either. We were scrambling at Foxtail today. Oh, hey, guys."

Mick turned to see Natalie and Wyatt joining them. Wyatt looked grumpy, but Mick had kept his word about no more kissing. Natalie, however, looked relaxed, if tired. "Sadie, are you telling Mick about the disaster in the bakery?"

"What happened?" Mick looked from Natalie back to Sadie.

"Some component died in the oven. Great timing, right?" Wyatt's chuckle held no mirth. "Dozens of Dove's pies were ready to bake, so every oven on the property has been running all afternoon. Mom's still baking at our house while she babysits Rose and Luna tonight."

"I'm amazed you made it here, with all that. I'd totally understand if you need to duck out and help Dove now that you've made an appearance." Mick didn't want Sadie to go, but pies were an essential part of Foxtail's income.

"Natalie did the math, and we can get them all baked in time this way." Sadie touched Mick's arm. "So don't worry, there will be enough for the post-nativity sale."

"I'm not worried about that as much as your livelihoods." Sadie and Wyatt had both confided in Mick how tenuous the finances were at Foxtail, and the cost of the oven repair wouldn't be cheap.

"One of these days we'll upgrade the equipment." Sadie sighed. "Your clinic isn't the only place in town that could use some updates."

True. Mick bit into a crisp red pepper while Leonard walked past, a loaded plate in hand. He loved the guy, but he couldn't help but feel frustrated by his unwillingness to invest in new equipment.

Then Mick felt convicted by his own, earlier words. "We were just talking about God's provision, weren't we? I need to trust in it."

"Speaking of providing in abundance." Natalie's eyes sparkled with mirth. "Did Sadie tell you about the poinsettias, Mick?"

"I haven't had the chance." Sadie shook her head at herself. "It's a doozy."

"The story will have to wait a minute, I think." Wyatt caught sight of something over Mick's shoulder. "Looks like Odette is trying to get our attention."

Sure enough, their hostess waved her hands. "If I may have your attention? I'm delighted to see you enjoying yourselves, but if I might have a moment of your time in the foyer, please?"

Mick wasn't sure how they would all fit in the entrance hall, but he placed a hand on the small of Sadie's back and guided her in that direction. They shifted for position among the other partygoers, facing the staircase, where Odette stood on the third or fourth stair from the bottom, visible to the gathered group.

She beamed down with her hands over her heart. "Look at all of you wonderful people. You, my friends, are true heroes, giving of your time and resources to help creatures who cannot speak for themselves. I thank you, one and all."

When the applause died down, Odette held up her hand. "Tonight is for you, so please enjoy the food and conversation. But first, will Sadie Dalton and Mick Larson join me up here?"

Mick blinked, caught off guard, but Sadie grinned as she tugged him forward. As if she'd known this was coming.

"What is this about? I haven't publicly announced Wade's donation."

"I might have mentioned it to Odette." She made a humorous cringing face. "Without naming names, of course. Why not share the news with everyone now and encourage them to attend?"

Public speaking wasn't his thing, but what choice did he have? This was an opportunity to spread the word, and they needed all the help they could get.

Once they were planted on the third stair, Mick cleared his throat. "Hi, I'm Mick from Goldenrod Veterinary Clinic, and as Odette said, it's encouraging to see so many people here tonight."

He spoke briefly about the overcrowded shelter's decision to treat every animal with dignity and kindness until they found their forever home. "Some of you—most of you, I hope—have seen advertising around town for a free-of-cost living nativity walk-through event, which will be held at Foxtail Farm on Saturday. What you might not know, however, is that the nativity is being made possible by an anonymous donor, who has also offered a substantial financial gift to the shelter."

Several gasps filled the air, along with murmured excitement.

"I hope you'll join us," Mick continued, "and also help

me extend my thanks to Sadie Dalton and her family at Foxtail Farm."

Once the applause died, Sadie's hands went to her heart. "We at Foxtail Farm are honored to host—but, friends, I have a confession to make. I am in big trouble."

She didn't look like it, the way her glossy lips turned up in a saucy smile, but Mick didn't dare take his gaze off her. What was going on?

"I have recently come into possession of five hundred poinsettia plants, which is four hundred and eighty more than I needed for the farmstand." Her patter was as crisp as a stand-up comedian's.

"Oh, Sadie." He wasn't sure whether to laugh or pat her shoulder in sympathy.

She kept smiling, though. "I won't tell you exactly how these poinsettias came into my possession, but let's say *someone* made a mistake the night she placed the order." She pointed at herself and cringed comically, making everyone laugh.

Mick hid a smile behind his hand, because even though this sounded like a big problem, Sadie had a knack of making lemonade out of lemons. He had no idea how she'd do it this time, but he was as eager as the rest of the group to find out.

"As some of you are aware, Foxtail Farm is donating all proceeds from the bakery to the shelter on Saturday night. I'd like to do the same with the poinsettia proceeds. They will all be placed around the farmstand, as well as on the path after the nativity experience, available for purchase. Who doesn't love a poinsettia plant at Christmas, especially if its purchase helps a worthy cause, right?"

A few people chuckled, but Sadie wasn't done.

"However, I believe we can make them extra special,

and to that end I'll be attaching a card to each plant—a trim tag—that features the name and photo of an animal in our shelter and other shelters in surrounding towns, to make it real just how many animals in our area deserve—need—homes. I can't promise it will lead to any adoptions, but it won't hurt. If anyone can help me in my time of need?" She lifted her hand to her forehead like a damsel in distress. "I'd be much obliged."

While the gathering laughed and clapped, Mick stared at her in awe. "You know I'm in. What do you need?"

"You're plenty busy, Mick." She spoke loud enough for all to hear, but her teasing words were just for him.

"I've got time," a voice called, to laughs. It was Alex, standing with a woman whose red hair and cheekbones identified her as his mom. "Tell me what to do, Sadie, and I'll do it."

"You're a peach, Alex." She called him out like an auctioneer making a sale. "Odette has offered to print up cards for the animals from our shelter, but I have yet to receive information from shelters in our neighboring communities. Once those cards are made, I'll need volunteers to help tie them onto the plants. But you know what? This is a party and I don't want to hold you all hostage, so if anyone else is interested, come find me tonight or just show up at the farmstand tomorrow after four."

Sadie couldn't take two steps from the staircase before being deluged. Alex was first in line, and Mick caught himself falling behind.

"It's exciting to see so much involvement, isn't it?" A tall man in his late fifties sidled up to Mick.

"It sure is." He thrust out his hand. "Mick Larson."

"Ivan Noll, in town visiting my nephew." He gestured toward Alex, still talking with Sadie.

"He mentioned you. You're a veterinarian, aren't you? Alex said your clinic partners with an animal shelter."

"Yes, and we're always eager to look for new ways to help animals. It sounds like you are too. Alex told me about your Valentine's human-pet speed-dating event." Ivan chuckled.

"I'll try just about anything to clear the shelter."

"Wouldn't we all." Ivan's eyes narrowed. "Alex says good things about how you've helped him with his Molly and how invested you are in the community. I'm impressed. It's difficult to juggle a veterinary practice with shelter work."

"I wouldn't want it any other way."

"Just the words I wanted to hear. In the new year, there will be an opening at my practice. I'd love for you to come check us out—a newly updated surgery suite, dedicated staff, a competitive salary and a shelter just yards away that needs promotion." Ivan pulled out his wallet and withdrew a business card. "Call or text anytime. We could use a go-getter like you on our team."

"Thanks, but—"

"Just think about it. I'll see you at the nativity."

"Sure, Ivan. Nice to meet you." He stuffed the card into his coat pocket.

It was more than half an hour before Sadie found him again. "What a fun party, isn't it?"

"A successful one, too, judging by the size of your smile. Did you get a lot of volunteers?"

"I did. Let's sit down for a minute. I've been on my feet all day." She crossed to a suede couch and lowered herself onto it, adjusting the silky fabric of her dress over her knees. "Are you upset I didn't run the poinsettia scheme past you before announcing it?"

"Hardly—but I'm concerned for you because Foxtail

won't make any money off them if the proceeds are donated."

"We'll break even once I subtract the wholesale cost, though. I don't care about making a profit if it goes to a good cause." She shuddered. "You should've seen us today when the truck dropped off five hundred of those babies. Right when I found out about Paul too—but like you said, we have to trust God to provide."

To emphasize her point, she gently thumped her hand on his leg, right above his knee. She seemed completely unaware of her action, but he was keenly mindful of it, how he wanted to place his hand atop hers and entwine their fingers.

He was glad he hadn't when her hand slipped away and she continued on, never seeming to have noticed what she'd done. "I can laugh about it now, which is good. How's your evening going? Anything interesting happen while we were mingling with other people?"

"I got offered a job. I think."

"What?" She spun sideways on the couch to gape at him.

"Or invited to apply by Alex's uncle. His clinic in Irvine partners with a shelter."

She hadn't moved a millimeter. "What are you going to do?"

"Stay here, of course. I promised my grandpa. My life is here. Why? Are you trying to get rid of me?" It was a joke, but he felt the pinch in his stomach that spoke to his deepest fears.

That he was never worth sticking around for, even by his friends.

"Of course not, you goof. I just know how dissatisfied you are with Leonard." She whispered the second sentence while looking around. "I don't want you to have any regrets."

"I would regret breaking my promise to my grandpa if

I left. Besides, I'm committed to providing free care to the shelter animals, and I'd like to find homes for more of them. Gidget too." He stretched his legs out in front of him.

"I'm surprised poor Gidget hasn't found a home yet, but I'll miss her when she gets a placement. So will Beatie, but we know Gidget is trained to do a job, and somewhere, someone needs her." She glanced at him. "I'm glad you're going to turn Ivan down."

He wished he didn't feel so relieved to hear her say so. "Good, because you're stuck with me. But I'd still like to learn more from Ivan about their clinic and shelter fund-raising."

"No doubt. But tonight, I think you've done more than enough to raise funds for the shelter. Odette told me she's received several checks."

"That's awesome."

She started to nod, but then her hand went to her mouth to cover a wide yawn.

"You've had a big day."

"A big bunch of days. This is our tenth date in thirteen days."

"Is it really?"

"You lost count?"

"I guess so. I've been having so much fun I stopped paying attention." He nudged her with his elbow. "This is the best December I've had in a long time."

She gave him the side-eye. "I never knew you were such a party animal, Mick."

"Haven't you had fun on our dates?"

"I have." Another yawn overtook her. "But I might need a cup of coffee to help me get through the rest of this one. No offense—it's not the company, I promise."

"Instead of coffee, let's get you back to Foxtail."

"I'm not sure Wyatt and Natalie are ready to go yet, though. They're making the most of having a babysitter."

"Why can't your date take you home?" He stood and extended his hand to her, hoisting her off the couch. "Come on, so you'll be well rested for the cast party tomorrow night."

"And luminaria making."

"And poinsettia-tag making." Whatever it was called.

Rather than let go of his hand, she squeezed it. "Has it really been a good December?"

"The best."

"That makes me happy. And sad, because I don't like thinking of you being gloomy at Christmas." She lifted his hand to envelop it in both of hers. "Next year, we'll make sure you go to plenty of parties."

"Sounds good." But it hadn't been all the events that had made it a memorable season. It had been the company.

Sadie.

This was the best Christmas he'd had in a long time—that he might ever have—so he intended to squeeze every last drop of fun out of their dating charade.

He didn't care if Wyatt was looking. He dropped a brief kiss on the crown of Sadie's head.

Chapter Ten

The day of the nativity dawned clear, cold and chaotic.

Last night's dress rehearsal, followed by the cast party, had been a blast, and Sadie was grateful that several of the cast members had come back this afternoon to help set up, including the replacements who had stepped up to take on the roles of Mary and Joseph.

Even though some of the cast looked hapless as they pitched in.

"There's a stretch of path with no poinsettias that way, Murray—other side. Thanks." Sadie gave the actor portraying one of the Magi a thumbs-up. "Looking nice, Glenda."

"I'm going to buy one of these yellow ones later." Glenda brushed off her hands. "The hue is so cheerful."

"I agree." Thankfully, a few of the other volunteers had expressed their intention to take home poinsettias too. Each sale would bless the animals in the shelter.

"Sadie? You just received a delivery." Mick strode toward her from the direction of the farmstand. Despite the cool temperature, he wore no jacket, and he'd pushed up the sleeves of both his flannel and the gray Henley tee he wore under it, revealing his strong, corded forearms.

She forced herself not to gawk. "It must be the Christmas roses."

Several guests at Blair's wedding had come in to purchase them, and she had sold out of most of them. Joining Mick to walk back to the farmstand, she noted the sweat on his brow. "What have you been up to?"

"Shoveling sand from a broken bag at the luminaria station. Setting up signs with Thatcher in the parking lot. And giving thanks that no matter what happens tonight, the animal shelter will be blessed. This expansion has been my goal for years now, and it's about to be met."

"That's something to celebrate."

"We will, once this is over. But for now, we still have work to do."

They avoided her workshop, where a few cast members helped scoop sand into paper bags for the luminaria, and entered the farmstand from the front entrance. Elena, in a black apron, dusted a display of holiday knickknacks. While Sadie found the delivery on the counter, she half listened to Mick and Elena talk about her donkey's participation in tonight's event.

"Speaking of Clover, my husband's expecting me to help bring her back over here. Is it okay if I leave now, Sadie?"

"Sure thing. We're closing the farmstand early today, anyway."

"Text me when you get here, Elena," Mick said. "I'd like to ensure Clover is settled all right."

"Got it." Elena removed her apron and hung it on a peg behind the register, where she gathered her purse. "See you soon."

"See you."

Mick held up his phone. "I need to respond to an email. Do you mind if I hang out here for a minute?"

"Of course not."

Sadie evaluated the Christmas roses in the delivery. Perfect. She switched them out for the remainder of her fading stock in the refrigerator, but in a moment of inspiration, she removed several stems. Why not share them in the office, where the volunteers would gather later for pizza? She placed them in a vintage white pitcher with some greenery.

"That's really nice." Mick tucked his phone in his jeans pocket. "It reminded me of that legend, where they're a gift of love to God. That's how I want to be, in everything I do. Thoughtful about serving God."

"I love that." Overcome by chills, Sadie rubbed her arms. "As much as I want Wade to be pleased, I don't want to forget why we decided to do the nativity. For the animal shelter as well as for the community. We wanted to share the story of the first Christmas."

"And now it's time to give it to God to use how He wants." Mick's touch on her shoulder was gentle, but it nevertheless sent sparks down her arm. "I'd better get back to the luminaria and then check on Clover when she gets here. But why don't I take these over for you first?" He glanced at the Christmas roses.

"That would be great, Mick. Thanks."

She let out a long sigh when he was gone. She had done a terrible job killing her attraction to him, and if anything, it was only getting stronger. And her feelings—

No. *Don't go there.* Thankfully, she had plenty to distract herself. She closed the farmstand, set the phone to voicemail and decided to check her email one last time before shutting down the computer.

One email was from the shop of the florist whose internship she had applied to back on Thanksgiving. Her nerves came alive as anxiety zipped through her, and her fingers trembled as she clicked on it.

She was glad there was no one in the farmstand to hear

her gasp. She was in! What a validation of her work. She had been noticed, accepted, invited. Her heart beat as fast as a hummingbird's.

"Sadie?" The deep, rich voice came from the workshop. It was Omar, one of the Magi, who had been crafting luminaria bags with Mick. "We're all finished, but we need to get home and clean up before coming back tonight, so we can't set out this last batch. Mick's checking on some sheep, I think. Can we leave this here?"

"Absolutely. I'll place the bags. Thank you so much."

Still shaking, she followed Omar into the workshop, where she loaded luminaria on her cart. Then, slowly, so as not to spill any, she pushed the cart toward the path.

"Ant Zadie!" The little cry was as sweet as it was insistent.

Sadie spun around to greet Rose and Luna, who were being pushed in a double stroller by Natalie. "Hello, my lovelies. Out for a walk?"

"No," Rose said. "We sitting, not wokk-ing."

"We wid-ing," Luna agreed.

"Riding in the stroller, yes." Sadie bit back a laugh.

Natalie's face was aglow with maternal affection. "I thought we'd see if there's anything we can do to help."

"Want to keep me company while I place the luminaria?"

"Sure." Natalie joined her and they started up the path, passing several already-placed luminaria that, along with wooden signs, would direct tonight's visitors from the nativity to the bakery. "These will look so pretty when they're lit up tonight. I can't wait to experience it with the girls."

"Hey, girl squad." Dove called from behind them. "I need a break. Can I come along?"

"Ant Duff, come." Luna wiggled in the stroller.

"Huwwy, giwl squad," Rose added.

"That settles it." After greeting the toddlers, Dove fell into step beside Sadie, putting a hand on the cart to help steady the bags. "Now that the ovens are working, I feel like I haven't left the bakery in two days. Have I missed anything new?"

"Just nativity prep," Natalie said.

"Actually, I have news." They had reached a bare spot on the path, so Sadie set the brake on the cart. "Do you remember the month-long internship I was going to attend when Dad passed away?"

"Vaguely." Dove scooped up two bags.

"Well, I was accepted to do it again next month."

Natalie reached out to hug her. "That's wonderful. I didn't know you had applied."

"I didn't expect to be accepted again since I had to turn it down once." She switched from Natalie's hug to Dove's. "Elena can manage the farmstand without me for a month."

"Of course she can, especially with our help. You deserve a little time away for yourself." Dove kissed her cheek. "As long as you're sure it'll be okay with the lawyer for you to be gone that long. We don't want to lose Foxtail Farm."

"I don't think this is any different than Natalie going on her honeymoon or you visiting Gatlin's family in Virginia. I'll double-check with the lawyer, but I'm sure the verbiage in Dad's will says we have to permanently reside on Foxtail Farm property, not that we can't take brief trips."

Natalie placed a luminaria bag. "I'm sure it's fine, but what about Mick?"

"What about him?" She didn't miss the way her sisters exchanged glances.

"This dating thing might be phony, but it's obvious there's something going on that's quite real." Dove clutched a paper bag to her chest. "You have feelings for him, don't you?"

She wanted to deny it, but…

She couldn't.

She tried not to have feelings for him. She didn't want to.

"It's complicated." She positioned a bag on the side of the path. "Someday soon I'll be able to tell you why we decided to date for December, but for now, the point stands that this relationship will be over soon. Regardless of any feelings I may or may not have."

"Maybe you two should talk. Reevaluate things."

"I'm not sure it would change anything—and honestly, it's possible that I've been swept away by the thrill of a December romance."

Even as she said it, though, she doubted it. Her relationship with Mick had deepened and grown. This was no lighthearted fancy.

Natalie glanced up from placing a bag. "This internship might be a good thing. The separation will give you both a chance to evaluate your friendship."

"Maybe, but I doubt time apart will change Mick's mind."

"You'd be surprised. Wyatt and I didn't speak for nine months, remember? We both changed a lot in that time." Natalie shrugged.

"I don't want Gatlin to change while he's gone from me." Dove frowned.

"You and Gatlin are committed, Dove." Sadie gave her sister a side hug. "As for me, I need to wait on the Lord."

"Maybe He'll provide you with an answer while you're in the internship. Or who knows, maybe even tonight." Natalie's attention returned to the girls, who were beginning to fuss. "I think we're about ready for naps. See you later?"

Sadie bent down to bid the girls goodbye. "Happy dreams."

Dove blew them kisses, and when the stroller was a few yards away, she checked her watch. "I'd better get back too."

"Don't forget, there will be pizza in the office at five. I ordered plenty for the cast and crew."

"Thanks for the reminder."

But once Sadie pushed the cart back to the workshop, she was so busy cleaning up and fielding questions from the cast that she didn't have time to get her own slice. As the sun set, she and a few teenage actors, including Kelsey, turned on the battery-powered candles in the luminaria.

It was fully dark and quite cold by the time she dashed back to her apartment to grab her Christmas-red scarf, hat and gloves. When she returned, the parking lot was full of cars.

Thank You for bringing people here, Jesus!

Eager to share the moment with Mick, she hurried out the door.

Mick grabbed a slice of pizza and savored the spicy sausage topping as he exited the Foxtail office. He hadn't been able to connect with Sadie the way he'd planned today, and he couldn't help wondering if she was as excited as he was.

Or as nervous.

Chewing, he hurried toward the area behind the farm stand where the cast and crew planned to meet twenty minutes before the nativity officially opened. From here, he could tell the parking lot was over half full—and whoa, there was a line of visitors standing at the nativity entrance too.

Thank You, God!

He jogged the rest of the way. Sadie was already with the group, bundled in her red hat and scarf, along with a few people who must be fresh recruits for tonight: Alex and his uncle, Ivan. Mick must be the last to arrive.

He pumped his fist in the air. "We've got a line of guests out front, people!"

The group erupted into cheers, but Sadie quieted them by raising her hand. "Let's make this quick. Thatcher, you're ready in the parking lot?"

"Yup, but I could use another person. That's why Alex is here."

"Thank you, Alex." Sadie nodded. "Wyatt?"

Wyatt hooked his thumb over his shoulder. "I'll do a security check now that there's a line, and my team will be active in and around the event. And Natalie says to tell you she and Dove are in the bakery. Pastor Luke is ready at his table to share resources about the first Christmas, and Odette is working the table for the animal shelter."

"Perfect." Sadie glanced up at Robin. "How's the cast?"

"We're ready, aren't we?" She led the amateur actors in a cheer.

"Then we're all set, I think." Sadie eyed Mick's pizza. "That looks so good."

"You didn't eat? Here."

She took the half slice from him without argument, chomped into it and offered it back.

"Gross." Thatcher smirked. "You're sharing food?"

Wyatt, as expected, scowled at Mick. But offering a hungry person his pizza was a far cry from kissing her.

There was no time to deal with his grumpy cousin, though. "I'm off to check the animals one final time."

"I could help." Ivan stepped forward. "It'll go twice as fast that way."

"You're on. Come with me." Mick led the older veterinarian to the side of the entrance gate, through the opening sets where the prophet Isaiah wrote of a coming Messiah and the Judean village where the Romans collected taxes. "If you wouldn't mind starting with the mares here—their names are Iris and Hyacinth—and work your way through to the sheep in the shepherd set, that would be great. It's a one-way path, but if you somehow get lost, the actors will guide you out. I'll start with the few sheep and Juniper's Labrador in the angel scene, and work my way through the manger and end with the camel at the wise men."

"Got it."

Mick was grateful for the help since they were running so short of time. Thankfully, the sheep seemed content and healthy, and Coco, Juniper's service dog, was calm. Juniper's foster mom, Bliss, wore a shepherd costume so she could be in the same scene, ready in case Juniper suffered an epileptic seizure.

Then he moved on to the manger scene. Clover the donkey nibbled hay under a costumed Elena's supervision, while the pygmy goats and sheep in the pen with her bleated at him.

Everything looked perfect—the animals, the sets and the cast, which included Dutch, Beatie, Glenda and the new recruits playing Mary and Joseph. He gave them a thumbs-up. "We're good to go."

"I quit!"

The yell made several people jump. Mick hurried from the manger set to the Magi's, where Murray was tossing his turban onto a hay bale.

"You can't quit." Omar scooped up the turban. "There were *three* wise men, Murray, not two."

Mick prayed for grace. "Murray, what's wrong?"

"I am a serious thespian, and I cannot be expected to

work in these conditions. That...thing?" He glared at Ike, the camel. "It's a menace."

"What do you expect? You're eating apple slices. Apples are one of his favorite treats." His handler, Leroy, stroked the camel's long neck. "I tried to warn you fellas not to bring snacks."

"I will not allow my life to be dictated by a camel. He was chasing me," Murray told Mick. "Look at how he's watching me."

Probably because you're causing a scene. And yeah, because you're not sharing. Mick gestured at a spot nearer the "star" spotlight. "Are you willing to eat your apples quickly, so this is no longer an issue? And stand over here so you aren't next to Ike?"

"I will not stay within fifty feet of that camel."

Leroy sighed. "Ike and I will leave, Mick. I don't want to cause trouble."

"Murray is already gone," Omar noted. Sure enough, Murray was halfway to the manger set, stripping off his costume as he went.

"This isn't your fault, fella," Leroy told Ike. "But what are we going to do now?"

Ivan trod onto the set. "I don't mind hanging out with a camel. I don't know the script, though."

"Leroy and I can handle it." Omar handed him Murray's turban. "You and Ike just stand there and look pretty."

Ivan stepped into the purple ensemble Murray had left behind. "I always wanted to be a wise man in the church pageant growing up, but I was always a shepherd. Oh, speaking of sheep, Mick? They're doing great. Plenty to eat and drink."

"Mick?" Glenda, clad in her homespun costume, beckoned him back to the manger scene. "It's Clover. Murray huffed through and she backed away from him. She scraped up one of her hind legs."

Mick jogged over to her, praying for wisdom. While this didn't sound like an emergency, it was far better to deal with an injury promptly to hopefully prevent infection.

At the manger set, several dour-faced cast members stood off to the side, watching Elena speak softly to Clover. The gray Sicilian donkey's large ears swiveled and her tail was tucked between her hind legs.

Mick let himself into the pen, skirting the sheep. "Elena, do you mind if I check her scrape?"

Elena sniffed. "Please."

"Here." Glenda appeared with two of Sadie's "ancient" lanterns. "They're not bright enough to perform surgery by, but hopefully they'll do."

"They're perfect, thanks." Just bright enough to offer him a good view. He approached Clover slowly, gently touching her fuzzy white snout, gaining her trust. Then he inspected Clover's right hind leg. "Thankfully, the cut isn't deep, but it's on the hock, which is a complex joint. Elena, you'll need to get in touch with your regular vet, but I'd still like to clean the wound, with your permission."

She nodded. "Anything to help her."

"What do you need?" Wyatt's deep voice came from behind Mick.

Mick hadn't realized his cousin had joined the group while he was inspecting Clover's leg. "Cold, clean water. Gauze and antiseptic. Topical ointment, if you have it."

"I've got those in the stable." Wyatt thumped Mick's shoulder. "I'll be right back."

"We'll meet you behind the farmstand," he called after him. The lighting was good there, and it would be far quieter, not to mention there would be visitors trekking through here any minute.

Slowly, Mick guided Clover from the manger set through to the Magi's set because it was the shortest route. Ivan broke ranks to call after him. "We heard about the donkey. Is she okay?"

He gave a brief rundown to his fellow veterinarian. "Elena will call her regular vet, but for now I want to cut the risk of infection."

"Good thinking. Hock injuries can be complicated." He turned away so others couldn't overhear him. "We could use someone like you in our practice. Don't forget to think about it."

Mick didn't need to think about it. He had promised to stay here. But this wasn't the time to talk shop. "I'm honored, Ivan. Truly. And thanks for pitching in last minute."

Ivan bowed. "My pleasure. These fellas are great. So is Ike."

The camel grunted.

Mick smiled. "See you after the show?"

"You've got it, Doc."

He and Elena slipped out and merged onto the path, where Glenda's husband, Calvin, waited to guide visitors down to the farmstand. He almost stopped in his tracks. "Wow."

"Isn't it something?" Calvin's thick white eyebrows wiggled. "Sadie outdid herself."

She sure had. The luminaria and poinsettia plants beautified the walkway in a way he could never have imagined. Sadie was a genius.

"This is gorgeous," Elena marveled. "So peaceful."

Clover seemed to be calmed by the gentle beauty of the scenery, too, appearing far more relaxed when they stopped behind the farmstand. Mick ducked into Sadie's workshop to wash up, and by the time he was finished, Wyatt had dropped off a box of supplies.

A few minutes later, Clover's wound was tended and her leg wrapped in a bandage. "You can take her home now, Elena. I'll check in tomorrow, but if anything changes tonight, call me or your regular vet." He gave her a list of things to look for.

"Thanks, Mick. I'm sorry there won't be a donkey in Bethlehem tonight."

"You'll both be missed, but Clover's well-being comes first."

He assisted Elena, then washed up again before hurrying out to the nativity's entrance. The line had grown in his absence. It was just now time for the event to open, and seeing him, Sadie brightened. "Everything ready?"

"Yes, after a few cast changes. Ivan is replacing Murray, and we're out a donkey." He briefly explained Clover's injury. "She'll be fine, but it's disappointing we're short a donkey."

"It's a crucial role at a nativity, isn't it? But what can we do?" Her lower lip caught between her teeth.

"Not a thing but be grateful Clover will be all right."

"You're right. Let's ask God's blessing." She shut her eyes and grabbed his arm. "Lord, thank You for this opportunity to share You with our neighbors. Please bless and protect everyone here tonight, heal Clover, and may this nativity glorify Your name. Amen."

"Amen." He smiled down at her. "Ready?"

"Ready." She turned to the first people in line. "Welcome to our living nativity. How many are in your party? Six? Come on in." She held up her hand to the next group. "We're spacing out parties every minute so it doesn't get overcrowded. I'll let you through shortly."

Over the next several minutes, numerous locals and out-of-towners entered the "stone" gate Aunt Jillian had made, their faces bright with excitement. But then he and Sadie were relieved of entry duty so they could help box up more pies, take photos of families in front of the John Deere and answer questions. The next two hours passed in a blur.

He had just finished loading four pink poinsettia plants in a woman's car when Thatcher waved at him, Sadie at his side. "I was just telling Sadie you two need to do the walk-through."

"And I keep telling Thatcher that we've been through dozens of times."

"Not while everyone is in costume." Thatcher gestured as Wyatt and Natalie approached. "Don't you think they should experience the nativity like the guests?"

Wyatt hesitated, but then he nodded. "It was moving when Natalie and I took the girls through. And you two deserve to see how it turned out."

"There are still a lot of people here, though." Mick glanced back at the buzzing bakery and farmstand area.

Wyatt waved them on. "Go enjoy the fruit of your labor."

"I have to admit, it would be cool to see it from start to finish." When Sadie looked at him with those dark eyes, he couldn't deny her a thing.

"It would." Mick offered his arm.

They took a slow pace, listening attentively to the actors' brief speeches. They had heard them multiple times in rehearsal, but experiencing it like this was different. Isaiah reading the prophecy of the future Messiah caused a lump in Mick's throat. Aunt Jillian's scenery, cleverly lit, looked almost real, especially when Caesar Augustus called for a census.

Glenda was quite impassioned delivering her lines about the difficulties of life under Roman rule, and when her helmet-wearing oppressors came to demand taxes, it was hard not to boo at them.

Sadie's three fabric tents off in the "shepherd's fields" of the meadow turned out amazing, with the artificial flames licking at the "campfires." Turning the corner to the angels' visit to the shepherds brought huge smiles while the kids sang out "Gloria in excelsis Deo."

Then, in the stable in Bethlehem, Mary and Joseph, as well as some shepherds and villagers, admired the doll in the manger. The white glow of a light behind the gauze curtain, another one of Sadie's ideas that had been beautifully executed to great effect, mimicked the Christmas star. And Dutch and Beatie, the innkeepers, sat off to the side with—

"Gidget?"

"I thought Gidget could be Clover's understudy." Sadie sounded thrilled. "After all, there are hundreds of poinsettias with the names of shelter animals who need homes. Gidget should be a part of this too."

"She seems to like the innkeepers better than she does Mary and Joseph," he murmured, thinking.

"Because Beatie gives her a lot of affection." Sadie waved at Beatie, who broke character to enthusiastically wave at them.

"You're a genius, Sadie." But one thing was missing. "I want to add something really fast. Will you wait here?"

"What?"

"Trust me."

He left Sadie open-mouthed by the manger and hurried through the wise men's set, glad to see Ike was contentedly chewing his cud.

He jogged back down the path. He wouldn't find any gold, frankincense or myrrh where he was going, but he hoped Sadie would appreciate his idea nonetheless.

***

Since there were no other visitors in the set, Sadie switched into the mode of organizer. "It's almost over. Are you all okay?"

"Perfect." Dutch gave her a thumbs-up.

"Gidget did a great job playing the donkey, didn't you, girl?" Beatie nuzzled the tiny horse's mane. "And she took good care of me too. I caught my toe on the edge of the manger, but she was right beside me, bracing me up, so I didn't fall."

"Wow." Sadie sent up a silent prayer of thanks that Beatie hadn't been hurt. If it hadn't been for Gidget being at the right place at the right time—

"Tonight has been so fun, and boy, have there been a lot of people." The girl playing Mary snuck a water bottle out from behind the manger and took a quick sip. "Next year, you need to do this for at least two nights. Maybe three."

All thoughts of Gidget whooshed out of her head. "This was a one-time thing, but…we'll think about it."

"I'm back." Mick emerged from the next set, breathing hard but not uncomfortably so. He carried—oh my, it was the milk pitcher of Christmas roses. "I hope you don't mind, Sadie, but considering the legend? I thought it would be okay."

"A gift of love." She watched as he set the pitcher beside the manger. The cluster of white blooms made a stark contrast to the browns of the straw and wooden set, but they fit.

The fact that Mick had remembered the legend didn't just warm her heart—it set it ablaze.

And she didn't want to quench the flames.

If she searched the world, she would never find a more giving, compassionate, wonderful man.

And he was the only man on earth she knew better than to fall in love with. Friends only—she had promised.

Lord, I want to be true to my word, but… I think it's too late.

Chapter Eleven

Mick and Sadie strode through the Magi scene, the nativity's last.

Did Sadie have any idea how amazing her ideas were for this? "The star, the curtain, everything was absolutely beautiful, Sadie—oh, hey, Calvin." Mick had forgotten Glenda's husband was stationed at the junction of the Magi's scene and the path to the farmstand.

"Hello, again." Rocking from one foot to the other, Calvin gestured at the path. "It's my job to tell you the poinsettias are for sale and the proceeds go to the shelter, but you know all that already. Besides, there don't seem to be too many flowers left. People have been grabbing 'em right up."

"I'm relieved and thrilled." Sadie mimed wiping sweat from her brow.

"The shelter will get a boon." On top of the generous check from Wade. Which reminded him—

"Sadie, have you seen Wade tonight?"

"Briefly. He was with a woman, but she was so bundled up I couldn't see her face."

"It must have been his neighbor." The one he'd wanted to do this for. "I hope he was pleased."

Calvin shrugged. "Who wouldn't be pleased? This was loads of fun."

"Thanks." Mick clapped his shoulder. "Well, Sadie, shall we?"

As pretty as the luminaria-lit path was, they kept a steady pace following the sounds of laughter and holiday tunes to the bakery and farmstand. Then Sadie pointed. "I see Wade."

Mick followed the direction of Sadie's gloved finger and found Wade holding a poinsettia plant in one arm and a pie box in the other, standing beside a woman seated on a hay bale. "Come with me?"

"Of course. I want to meet his special friend."

"Wade." Mick reached for the pie box as soon as they were within a few feet. "Let me help you with that."

"Ah, the couple of the hour."

"I would say that's you and—is it Cassandra, ma'am?" Mick extended his hand to her.

"That's correct." With bright eyes and delicate features, she was a lovely woman, but her grip was weak. "Mick Larson and Sadie Dalton, I presume?"

"Lovely to meet you." Sadie took her hand after Mick let go. "We understand you experienced a living nativity some time ago. Was it like this one?"

"In many ways, especially in the reverence to God, which is the most important thing. I enjoyed myself immensely, and I'm so grateful to Wade for bringing me."

Wade looked down at Cassandra with unabashed affection. "It was my honor."

Sadie grinned at Mick.

Wade seemed to remember they were there and, flustered, forced a smile. "I appreciate the hard work of the cast and crew, but you two bore the brunt, I'm sure."

"We had fun." Sadie wasn't good at accepting thanks, but she wasn't wrong. "We always have fun when we're together."

There was something in the way she said it that made Mick's stomach swoop. Did her words extend to the kiss they'd shared?

Did she ever think of it? He certainly did. More often than he should.

He cleared his throat. "This wouldn't have been possible without you, Wade."

"I'd do it again in a heartbeat. Pastor Luke was able to speak to several individuals about the nativity, and I pray that everyone who came will think about what they experienced tonight."

"I'll do the same." Now it was Cassandra's turn to smile sweetly at Wade.

Huh. Maybe they were no longer just friends and neighbors. But at the same time, Mick observed faint lines of tension marring Cassandra's features. He recalled that she had just undergone treatment for an illness, and she must be weary. He wouldn't keep her out in the cold any longer. "Were you on your way out? I'd be happy to carry these for you."

Wade shook his head. "Thank you, but that rancher friend of yours is bringing the car closer for Cassandra."

"Thatcher's my cousin, and an excellent driver." Sadie sat beside Cassandra on the hay bale. "While you wait, would you like a hot mug of apple cider?"

"Thank you, dear, but I see the car coming now." Cassandra allowed Sadie to assist her to stand. "I've been ill, as I suspect you know, but this trial has taught me to grab hold of the good things in life. Tonight has been a good thing. And so has Wade's faithful companionship. How many people take the time to know you so well they give you the perfect gift?"

As Thatcher pulled up in Wade's white sedan, Mick assisted Cassandra into the passenger seat. "Good advice, Cassandra."

"I wish I'd learned it sooner. Then I wouldn't have wasted so much time."

"Thank you again, Mick." Wade's handshake was firm. And then they were gone.

He and Sadie watched their red taillights grow smaller as they drove away. Then Sadie sighed. "She's so fragile. I wonder if Gidget would be a good match for her. To help her with her balance?"

"Possibly, but I don't know enough about Cassandra's condition. If she recovers completely, she won't have need of a service animal once she regains her strength." Mick turned around, ready to tackle the next thing on the list. They wouldn't do a full teardown of the nativity sets until Monday, but there was still a lot to do, and scores of people were still bustling around the farmstand.

Including Aunt Jillian and Uncle Gary, posing for a photo with Wyatt, Natalie and the twins in front of the tractor.

Sadie nudged him with her elbow. "Are you okay?"

"Yeah, just thinking." Hurting a little, too.

"Do you want to walk with me to turn off the luminaria candles? I thought they looked good, for being run by batteries."

"Everything looked good," he said as they strode back to the path. "I'm floored by how well this went despite all the commotion we experienced going into it. I mean a set fell down, we lost our Mary and Joseph, then right before showtime a wise man quit and Clover got injured—great job bringing in Gidget, by the way."

"She's a natural." Sadie walked past the luminaria. "Let's start at the far end. I think your aunt's crew already shut down the set lights, and I'd rather walk toward the lights of the farmstand than away from them."

"Smart." To his relief, there weren't more than six or seven poinsettia plants left. He'd be sure to buy them all before he left tonight.

"Something else happened before the nativity. Something wonderful." She clutched her hands to her chest. "Do you remember that I was scheduled to attend a brief internship in Los Angeles back when my dad died?"

"Not the specifics, but I recall the situation." She'd had to choose between her career and her family keeping Foxtail Farm. "You were so excited about that opportunity."

"I was, and it's not the sort of thing that happens every year. But there's another one for the month of January, and guess what? I was accepted."

She looked so ecstatic, so vibrant, his heart could burst. He hugged her, then pulled back. "That's fantastic, Sadie. I'm so happy for you. Tell me more about it."

She danced ahead to kneel beside a luminaria. "I leave New Year's Day, and I'll stay with my friend Ruth—do you remember her? She used to work with me at Goldenrod Floral Designs."

"Sure, I remember. Sounds like you'll have a blast hanging out." As he shut off a candle, he realized how much he would miss her. "Will you be too busy for me to visit one weekend?"

"Weekends are when I'll be busiest, I'm afraid." The plastic candle in her hand grew dark with a click of the switch. "The other interns and I will assist for weddings and parties, which are almost always on weekends. Plus, there are daily orders at the shop. It'll be a lot of work, but I'll learn so much. And it's only four weeks, so it won't cause any issues with Dad's will."

At least it was only for a month. He'd gladly pay the price of missing her for her to have such a fantastic opportunity. "No one deserves it more than you, Sadie."

Another faux candle went out in her hand. "I don't know about that, but it will be good for me to be exposed to new trends, network with others in the industry, that sort of thing."

"It's a great opportunity." He clicked off another candle. "You know, maybe we should've collected these and then turned them off back at the farmstand."

"We'll do that next year." How could a smile be audible? But hers was.

"We're doing this next year?"

"Maybe." *Snick*. Another candle went out. "Anyway, I'll come back in February with so many ideas that will serve us well at Foxtail. And help me start my own business. Wherever that will be."

Mick flicked a candle switch so hard his thumb screamed. "What do you mean, 'wherever'? You can't leave Foxtail Farm."

"Not until the five years are up on the will. Then I'm free to open a shop." She set down the bag in her hands without turning off the candle within. "You know that's what I've always wanted."

"Yeah, but you're staying in Goldenrod, though, right?"

"And rent space downtown, next door to Goldenrod Floral Design? I wouldn't last a month."

Was this panic battering at his chest? "It doesn't have to be downtown."

"Where could it be, then? I can't exactly see my family letting me have space for my own business on Foxtail property once we're free to make changes to how we run things. I doubt they'll see flowers as an integral part of the business." She grimaced. "I'm sorry, I don't mean that. But they talk about expanding the bakery and the ranch and building more cabins, never about making floral design part of how we do things here. I just want to start over sometimes, Mick. Does that make sense?"

"No."

In the golden light of the luminaria, her face hardened. "No?"

"All this time, I knew how much you sacrificed for your family. But I didn't realize that meant you would leave when you were free to." He strode toward her, his emotions so jumbled and intense that every muscle was taut, every nerve fiber quaking with...

Fear.

"I don't want you to go, Sadie."

Her mouth was open in surprise as she looked up at him, her long lashes fluttering over eyes dark and wet as spilled ink.

He didn't think. Just wanted to douse the fear burning through him.

His hands cupped her neck. Held her head. Waited the span of a breath for her to pull back, but she didn't. She leaned forward, into him.

So he kissed her.

And didn't want to let go.

Sadie had never felt like this before.

The only other real kiss she and Mick had shared had played to a crowd, for public consumption. It might have made her heart race, but it was for show.

This kiss was completely different.

It was tender. Warm. And it felt oh, so real.

When they broke apart, she rested her cheek against his

chest, listening to his pounding heart. Everything about this moment was so precious. She wanted to commit it to memory.

How could this be any more perfect? She and Mick fit like interlocking jigsaw pieces, not just in their gentle embrace, but in the way they shared their lives.

Their dates may have started out as fake as spray-on snow on a Christmas tree, but Sadie's long-denied attraction could no longer be ignored. Nor could her feelings. He was drawn to her, too, otherwise he would not hold her so tenderly, as if afraid to let her go.

Friends didn't kiss like this. Hug like this. And, like it or not, there was no going back. It was time to step out from feeling like the ignored middle child and into something bright and beautiful.

She had never been less than honest with him. She wouldn't start now.

"Mick, we work well together, don't we?"

His Adam's apple worked against the top of her head. "You mean the nativity?"

"No. I mean us." She took a fortifying breath of icy air. "I don't feel like just friends anymore."

She felt his emotional withdrawal before he stepped out of her arms. "Sadie, no."

She would feel like a fool, except now that he had shared more about his upbringing with her, she understood this wasn't about her. The barrier around Mick's heart had been built over years and years, fortifications to protect himself from pain.

And he didn't just want to protect himself. He wanted to protect her, too, because all the love he had given in his younger years—to his aunt and uncle, and the few romantic relationships he had allowed himself—hadn't been reciprocated.

How could he trust? He might view himself as unlovable.

She couldn't, wouldn't, let him believe that.

"I know you're afraid, but Cassandra said something tonight that hit me. About how well Wade knew her and how he gave her the perfect gift. She also said we have to grab hold of the good things in life and not take them for granted. This, what we have?" She gestured between them. "It's more than friendship. More than chemistry. We trust each other. We're always there for each other. You know me better than anyone, Mick, and I know you. Enough to recognize how much love scares you."

"Love?" It came out ugly. "If you know me so well, then you know why I can't be with anyone."

"I'm not anyone, Mick. I'm your best friend."

"And I care about you too much to inflict myself on you. I will never bring another person into the mess that is my life."

"Isn't it the other person's choice too?"

His features hardened. "I can't love you, Sadie. I'm sorry, but it's for the best, because I could never make anything good come out of a relationship."

Rejection spread through her, hot and thick, but she wouldn't allow him to believe such falsehoods about himself.

"You were let down as a child. Your mom was sick, and I have compassion for her. But I wish she had overcome her struggles and been able to keep you so you could have felt her love every single day of your life, the way you deserved. She did the best she could, giving you to Jillian to raise, but how could you not have problems trusting that love is safe when you never knew when she was coming back?"

"She wasn't the only adult in my life, Sadie."

"You're right. I wish your dad hadn't run off before getting to know what an incredible, amazing son he had. I wish your aunt and uncle hadn't made you feel second rate. Even your grandpa couldn't express love in words. But that doesn't mean you're not worthy of it, Mick. You deserve unconditional love."

"That only exists from God."

"Yes, but I don't believe that makes human love any less important in our lives. There's so much love around us to remind us what love can do. Wyatt and Natalie. Dutch and Beatie—"

"I am not made for it." His eyes were black as night. "This is proof. I never wanted to hurt you, never wanted to lose you, but I've ruined everything letting this go too far. I should never have kissed you like that just now. It was reckless and selfish."

She refused to be hurt. "I'm glad you did. Those kisses helped clarify things for me."

"Well, they muddled my vision, because I should have seen this coming. Every time in my life that I've let down my resolve and think *Okay, maybe I can have love*, I get shut out. My aunt and uncle can't love me, but at least they haven't lied, because everyone who uses the *L* word with me leaves me sooner or later. My mother. The relationships I had when I was younger." His eyes grew cold. "Even you."

"I'm not—" Her heart stopped beating. "Oh. Because I said I'd leave Goldenrod."

"All this time, you've been planning on moving away as soon as the terms of your dad's will are fulfilled. You never intended to keep me around as part of your daily life."

"But, Mick, I won't leave if we are together—"

"You're implying I would be enough to make up for dissatisfaction in your career?" His scoff chilled her.

"God would provide something. You are enough for me, though, Mick, and more. Don't tell me the past few weeks haven't meant something to you. Not just the kisses. We were vulnerable with each other, more so than we've ever been. We've grown together. What we have is special. It's love."

"No, it's a mistake. You knew the rules when we started this. December only. I'm sorry Sadie. Sorrier than I can say. But I can't give you what you want. I don't deserve it."

"Yes, you do!" She stomped up to him and made him look at her. "You deserve love, Mick Larson. How am I going to drive that into your gorgeous but very thick skull?"

He stepped back, his eyes hard. "I can't risk believing you. It hurts too much when things fall apart. Eventually, you'd regret wasting your time on me."

"I'm never going to regret a single moment we spend together." The fact that he didn't return her love caused a pain plunging into her like a knife to the ribs, but nothing he said or did, even failing to love her, could kill her love for him. "And no matter where I am in the universe, I will be there for you. Nothing has changed, and I won't stop being your friend."

"Everything has changed. Our friendship no longer exists, Sadie."

She'd thought the pain in her ribs was agonizing, but now it hurt so much that she struggled to breathe. "Am I Is it too hard to be friends with me? I'm living in Goldenrod for more than two years before Dad's will is satisfied. Shouldn't we try to work past this?"

"There's no way past this." He turned away, ruffling his hair.

"Our lives are so entwined. Can't we try?"

"That's futile." He turned back, unable to meet her gaze.

"I'll make it easy on us. Alex's uncle offered me a job in Irvine, and I'll take him up on it."

"But...you're a partner in your grandpa's clinic. You promised him—"

"I have to break that promise. I'm so frustrated fighting the old tech at the clinic, and as long as Leonard is senior partner with the greater share, we're falling further behind in patient care. My grandpa would understand why I'm going."

It made perfect sense, but she didn't believe he would be leaving if she hadn't told him how she felt. Should she have kept her mouth shut? Being honest with him had backfired. So badly that he was going to walk away from his family, his friends and the veterinary practice he dreamed of running someday.

Then she saw the flash in his eyes. "You're not leaving because of the clinic. Or because you can't bear the sight of me anymore. It's because you do care about me."

His eyes hardened, as swift and harsh as a slammed door. "I hope you find what you want, Sadie. I'm sorry it can never be me."

And with that, he skirted past her down the path, leaving her utterly alone.

Chapter Twelve

"Thank you so much for coming by today. Merry Christmas." Sadie waved farewell to the customer, an abashed-looking man in his forties who'd run through the farmstand with the speed of a contestant on one of those shopping-themed game shows. He'd grabbed a few hundred dollars' worth of apple butter and jams, candles, cookbooks and poinsettias without much rhyme or reason.

"Do you think he forgot to do his Christmas shopping until now?" Elena joked as she swung the open sign hanging on the door to *Closed*.

"I got that impression." Sadie cringed. "But that's almost the last of the poinsettias." They wouldn't sell anymore. Like many businesses in town, Foxtail Farm closed at noon on Christmas Eve. The rest of the day was for family. Church. Friends.

But Sadie wasn't sure she'd see her best friend later today. Mick had all but disappeared from her life.

Lord, I don't think I made a mistake telling him, but I need Your help to reconcile with him. We're connected through Wyatt and Natalie, Rose and Luna, church...

"The outgoing deliveries are ready. I'm happy to take them. The nursing home is on my way, anyway." Elena gestured at the two tiny decorated trees scheduled to go out today.

"Sure, but just a minute." Sadie gathered the last two holiday arrangements from the cooler. Then she grabbed a pen and piece of notepaper.

Please share with anyone who finds themselves alone today.

Alone.

Was Mick alone? Right now? In a way, he had been alone his entire life in a world where he believed he was unlovable.

She glanced at Elena as she removed her apron. "Do you have one more minute? I want to send flowers to someone who's never received them before. I think he might appreciate it."

"Gotcha." Elena turned away, but Sadie caught a glimpse of her smile anyway. Clearly, she had a good guess who the flowers were for. "I'll load these into my car while you put it together."

"Take the last of the poinsettias too. One for you, one for your mom."

"Ooh, thanks." Elena scooped the pots into her arms.

Sadie slipped into her workroom and selected a wide, clear glass vase. Alongside the last of the Christmas roses, she tucked in bay laurel, pine sprigs and a pick of gold and white holiday baubles.

Her hands shook the whole time, but she was practically quaking when she started to write on the card. Her handwriting was so bad she threw her first attempt into the recycling bin and tried again with a larger card so she could fit everything in.

After signing her name, she added a quick postscript.

I plan to tell Beatie and Dutch the truth tonight.

There. Now Mick could join in the conversation if he

wanted. After all, he was invited to Wyatt and Natalie's party. The rest of his family would be there. And now he wouldn't be blindsided when she pulled Dutch and Beatie aside.

She attached the card just as Elena returned. "Perfect timing."

Elena studied the address on the card, then nodded. "I'm glad you found a use for these before they fade. I hate throwing out flowers."

"Me too." In fact, she could have given away a lot more flowers this Christmas season if she'd had more vases. She'd never considered asking for donations, but maybe—

"I'll see you tonight at church." Elena's words drew Sadie from her reverie.

Sadie hugged her sideways so as not to disturb the floral arrangement. "Thanks again for making the deliveries."

Sadie locked the door behind Elena, then turned off the Christmas tree lights and the music on the sound system. Once she finished tidying the workshop, she had a checklist of things to accomplish before the party tonight. Presents to wrap, a casserole to bake and trying her best not to think about Mick's response when he received the Christmas roses.

Dove shoved open the back door, her phone in her hand. "Did you see the group text from Dutch yet?"

Sadie's stomach sank. "My phone's in my purse. What happened?"

"Beatie fell this morning and had to go to the urgent care. They're on their way home now, but he's asking if you, Natalie and I can come to the house now. It must be serious if they want us over to talk."

Since Dove and Natalie still didn't know Beatie was undergoing tests, Sadie suspected Dutch's text indicated he and Beatie were ready to share. Maybe they even had a diagnosis now. Her heart pounded an anxious beat, but she took a deep breath. "It's a good sign that she wasn't sent to the hospital, but I'm concerned about her."

"Me too. I'll text Natalie to meet us at Beatie's house." Dove stepped toward the door. "Give me a second to grab something from the bakery for them, and we can go."

"I'll drive." The minivan was right outside.

Sadie snagged a tree-shaped rosemary plant and a holiday basket packed with soup and muffin mix off the shelf. With a quick stop for her coat and purse, she made it to her car in record speed.

She would need God's strength even more if she were losing Beatie on top of Mick's friendship.

Mick checked Pal's vitals one more time, then gave the gray-whiskered German shepherd a rub between the ears. "I'd warn you to stay away from mistletoe in the future, buddy, but I think you got the picture. The thought of mistletoe makes me nauseated too."

Pal looked up at him with soft brown eyes that expressed complete agreement.

Thankfully, Glenda and Calvin's poor pup hadn't consumed any of the plant, but in an attempt to keep him away from it, Calvin had fallen into the Christmas tree. He was fine, but Pal had stepped on a shattered ornament.

Mick left Pal to rest and made his way to the clinic's waiting room, where Glenda and Calvin sat in the creaky blue chairs, heads bent together as if praying.

As soon as he crossed the threshold, they broke apart and stood. "How's our boy?"

"The cut is stitched up. He'll be just fine."

Glenda wiped away a tear, and Calvin chuckled in relief.

"You know what'll prevent this sort of catastrophe from happening in the future, honey?"

"Plastic ornaments?"

"Well, yes, but I was going to say fake mistletoe." Calvin wagged his finger.

The word *fake* bit at Mick like a mosquito. Like mistletoe, it reminded him of Sadie. Fake dating. Kisses beneath the mistletoe and on the path.

And he didn't want to think of her, because he had hurt her. He would never forget the wounded look in her eyes as long as he lived.

In the four days since the nativity, he had worked overtime to avoid her. He went to the first service at church on Sunday morning because she'd be at the second service, and he helped Aunt Jillian tear down the nativity sets while he knew Sadie wouldn't be home. On Monday, he checked on Gidget before opening the clinic, and when he swung by Foxtail to tend to Gidget on the way home, the farmstand was already dark.

He missed Sadie, but this was how it had to be.

Glenda's hug dragged him back to the present. "I'm sorry you had to work past noon on Christmas Eve."

"I don't mind at all." He had stayed after the clinic closed to write his resignation letter after Leonard and Glenda left, anyway. Good thing he was here, since poor Pal had required emergency care.

"Sadie must be wondering where you've gotten to." Glenda's hands went to her heart. "You two are the cutest."

Mick hadn't uttered a word about his failed faux relationship with Sadie. They had planned to stay together until Beatie was settled with a diagnosis, and since it was already Christmas Eve, Beatie might not know anything until after the New Year.

He would have to make up some excuse as to why he couldn't make it to Wyatt and Natalie's party tonight.

But for now, he offered instructions for Pal's aftercare and sent the dog home with Glenda and Calvin with wishes for a mistletoe-free Christmas.

The exact same type of Christmas he'd be having himself.

Before he locked up, he set the resignation letter on Leonard's desk, where the senior partner would find it Monday morning.

"Come, Fly."

With a jingle of her tag, his faithful companion hopped from her bed in his office, her paws making tip-taps on the linoleum floor. They got into his frosty truck and drove straight to Manzanita Ranch.

Once he arrived, he carried so many wrapped packages to the front door that he had to ring the doorbell with his elbow.

Aunt Jillian grinned and admitted him into the richly decorated home. Fly trotted toward her, stopping for a brief pat before disappearing into the house. "What a surprise. You've missed your uncle, though. Last-minute shopping. I think he secretly likes all the hustle and bustle on the twenty-fourth."

The aroma of baking cranberry bread took him right back to his childhood Christmases. It should have been a happy feeling, but today, it felt like a kick in the gut.

"Speaking of presents, I thought I'd drop these off."

"You know the way to the tree."

He sure did. He found Fly in the living room, making herself comfortable on the rug before the empty hearth. He deposited the presents off to the side of the professionally decorated tree. That way, his aunt could place them exactly where she wanted them. "They're all here, gifts for you and Gary, Wyatt and Natalie, and the girls."

"Smart of you to bring them by now. One less thing for you to worry about tomorrow morning."

He prayed for strength. "I'm not coming tomorrow. Or to the party tonight."

Her thin eyebrows rose. "Are you ill? Sit down, and I'll make you a honeyed tea."

"No, I'm fine. That way, anyway." All of a sudden, he felt five years old again, out of place in this immaculate home, yearning for something he couldn't have.

"Are you tired, then? It's a pretty day. Why don't you head over to the stables and take one of the horses out for a ride? It'll perk you right up."

It was a kind offer, but Mick recognized it as a deflection. Tough topics weren't discussed at the Teague home, but there was no avoiding this one.

"No, thank you. I'm sorry Uncle Gary is out so I can't tell you both at the same time, but I've been offered a job in Irvine." He shoved his hands into his jacket pockets. "I thought I belonged here, but I've been fooling myself."

"Of course you belong in Goldenrod. You have your grandfather's veterinary practice."

"I don't mean Goldenrod, Aunt Jillian."

Her eyes narrowed. "You're talking nonsense, Mick."

It felt like he was trying to swallow around a golf ball. "I'm so grateful to you and Uncle Gary for taking me in. Time and again, whenever my mom relapsed. Even though I'm not really a member of *your* family, you and Uncle Gary and Wyatt? You were mine. You *are* mine. And before I leave town, I want you to know that I love you."

"Not a member of our family?" Aunt Jillian's cheeks paled.

"You used those words with Wyatt, when we were eight or so."

"I don't remember saying it, but I couldn't have meant

that you weren't part of *the* family." The words came out in a rush. "I was probably trying to reassure Wyatt. He was a child, and your leaving and coming back confused him. But you're one of my boys, Mick. You know how we felt about you. Surely that counts for more than something I said decades ago. Nothing but words."

"Words that wounded, and they were backed up by actions. From excluding me from family photos, all the way up to your Thanksgiving comment about Rose and Luna calling me *uncle*. You wanted me to know where I stood in this family, and I do."

"No." She reached for him, her hands cold as snow. "Mickey, I'm sorry."

"I don't blame you for not loving me, Aunt Jillian. I was a broken kid dropped on your doorstop, but you went above and beyond to give me a stable home. I have nothing but appreciation for all you did for an unwanted kid like me."

Her chin trembled. "You were wanted. Always."

Mick's heart thumped, even though he didn't dare believe her. "Why couldn't you have told me you wanted me, then, even if you couldn't love me? I brought it up to you so many times, but you never grasped the opportunity to reassure me."

"Mickey, when you came to me all of five years old, you were so vulnerable, so confused. I didn't want to make it worse for you, because the plan was for your mom to come back and get you when she finished rehab. I knew I would have to let you go, and I did. But then you came back, and the cycle repeated. It broke my heart every time Monica came for you."

How could this be true? She'd never shown an inkling.

"It hurt so much," she continued, her breath hitching, "it was easier to hold you at a distance. I was protecting myself,

I see that now, but I was also trying to protect you. I didn't want you to know how hard it was for me to give you up each time. And we chose to put on a brave face, never talking about anything upsetting, so you wouldn't know how distraught we were. Gary doesn't like to talk about difficult topics, anyway, but I thought avoiding it would benefit you." She sniffled. "The last thing I wanted to do was turn you against your mother. But I suppose the last thing I *should have* wanted was to make you feel unloved."

He had never seen her cry before. The Teague home was not a place for tears. But she began to sob, and crumpled against him.

His arms went around her thin frame. "It's okay, Aunt Jillian."

"It was the most painful thing I've ever been through in my life, giving my son—you—back to his mother."

After that, he couldn't understand the rest of her words through her sobs. A healing peace flowed through him, though, now that he had a better understanding of why his aunt had treated him as she had. *Thank You, God. Please heal our hearts and strengthen our bonds.*

When her tears quieted, Aunt Jillian pulled back, patting his arms as if she were still not entirely comfortable with expressing her feelings. That made two of them, but he was grateful she was trying along with him.

"Will you sit down for a minute? I want to know how Sadie feels about you taking a job out of town."

Mick sat on the couch, patting Fly as she settled at his feet. "We were better as friends. We never should have messed with it." Not even to placate Beatie and Dutch in a difficult time.

"Oh." Aunt Jillian bit her lip.

"Yeah." No need to elaborate. His aunt clearly understood

that the relationship was as lifeless as the last few brown leaves clinging to the crepe myrtle tree outside the window.

"I thought that tough shell around your heart was because those two girls you dated hurt you too deeply, on top of your mother not being…well, stable." She sat in a chair across from him. "But I now see that I hurt you the most. Nevertheless, I hoped when you and Sadie started dating, it was a sign that you had healed up."

Was a broken heart the sort of thing that ever healed perfectly? With God's grace, yes, although he suspected his heart would always bear fault lines along the fractures as reminders. "I'm meant to be alone. I always knew that, so dating Sadie was a mistake."

She eyed him with blatant curiosity. "Why did you choose to, then?"

"A long story that I'll tell you later." Beatie and Dutch should hear it first. "But I hate how I've hurt her."

"She must be heartbroken. She loves you deeply."

His hand went still on Fly's back. "How did you know?"

"Anyone with eyes can see it. Can't you?"

"I don't think I wanted to see it."

"Whyever not?"

He and his aunt had never talked like this before. Ever. It felt strange but, at the same time, soothing. Like he had been waiting to speak like this with her for a long time, the way he'd always imagined other people talked to their moms.

He'd already been vulnerable. He might as well go all in.

"Because I knew it would end. It always does. My mom tried to stay for me but couldn't, and I've never been enough for anyone I dated." He stared at the floor. "They all said they loved me, but they left. I didn't ever want Sadie to leave me, so it stands to reason I don't want her to love me."

"She's not leaving, honey. She's bound to Foxtail Farm by her dad's will."

"Only for a few more years, but once her time is up, she's moving away. She might say she loves me, but just like with everyone else, she has no problem taking off."

Although that wasn't quite fair. She had a career at stake.

"Did she say all of that, or are you assuming it? By the look on your face, I'm guessing you are jumping to some conclusions."

"I don't think it's a big jump."

"I understand why it's difficult for you to trust, Mick. Love can be scary because it requires you to open your heart to the possibility of pain. But you and Sadie are not like your parents, or like me and Gary. You're on your own path. If you don't want to live without Sadie, don't let her go. I can see how much she cares for you—and well, I know you care for her too."

Not in that way. Did he?

Their friendship was deep and strong, sure. But add in their kisses, and—

He had never allowed himself to be fully honest about how they had affected him.

Nor had he realized that his care for Sadie might be rooted in something deeper than friendship.

Maybe he should go out to the stable and take a ride after all. There was something appealing about the idea of being out among the pines with a horse and dog for company while he prayed for guidance.

His cell phone buzzed in his pocket. "Excuse me a sec. It could be the clinic's answering service about an emergency." But it was Leonard Coggins's name on the screen.

Had he come back to the clinic and found Mick's letter?

It would have to wait, however, because he had missed

two texts from Wyatt, sent several minutes apart. The first text bubble was a question about Gidget's feed, but the second had him on his feet.

"I'm sorry, Aunt Jillian, but it's Beatie. She fell."

"I'm sorry to hear that. Is she at home or the hospital in La Mesa?"

"Home, thankfully." And with a diagnosis. "Sounds like she'll be okay, but I just realized something, and there are a few things I need to do before end of day. Come, Fly." Then he did something he hadn't done in years. He instigated a hug with his aunt, knowing it would be welcomed.

"I love you," she whispered.

He let the words sink into his bones before he let her go. "I love you too."

Chapter Thirteen

Sadie sat squished between her sisters on Beatie's denim couch, her heart in her throat. Beatie sported a blooming bruise on her hand from catching her fall earlier this morning.

Sadie hated to think of the other bruises on Beatie's body. "Are you in pain?"

"A pinch, but from the tumble I took down the stairs, not from the macular degeneration."

"I'm so sorry you've been going through this for weeks and we never knew." Dove shook her head. "I understand your choice not to say anything, though."

Dutch met Sadie's gaze, as if asking her to continue to keep quiet about her knowledge of Beatie's difficulties. For the time being, at least. Her nod was tiny, but she could tell he caught it.

Natalie shifted on the couch. "What a blessing that your test results came in while you were at the doctor's office. Otherwise, you might have had to wait for word until after Christmas."

Beatie settled back in her chair beside the wood-burning stove. "At least I have a diagnosis now. I never would've thought macular degeneration could not only cause vision problems but wreak havoc with my balance too. I knew my eyesight wasn't what it once was, but I chalked it up to my age or stress or needing new glasses."

"No one wants to hear a diagnosis like this, but I'm relieved we have an answer." Dutch stood and kissed the top of his wife's head. "I'll fetch you a blanket."

"Thanks, sugar." This close to the stove, Beatie couldn't be too cold, but Sadie was of the opinion that a cozy blanket always made things better.

She reached for Beatie's warm, calloused hand. "I'm so sorry, Beatie. How can we help?"

"Just pray and love me. The doctor will help us work out the rest."

"In the meantime, I brought you some apple turnovers," Dove said. "Would you like one with a cup of coffee?"

"Sounds delicious, Dove my dear, but not now." Beatie's smile was sweet. "I think I'd like to rest my eyes so I can go to the party and church tonight."

Dutch returned with the blanket. "I'm not sure we'll be up to going out tonight, hon."

"We'll see." Beatie's tone brooked no argument.

Sadie hesitated to rise from the couch with her sisters. She wanted to talk to the Underhills and tell them the truth about her relationship with Mick. Everyone would realize they weren't together tonight, anyway, and Sadie didn't want them hearing it through gossip.

But Beatie shut her eyes, and Sadie could only pray for God to provide another opportunity.

"We'll let you rest." Natalie kissed Beatie's cheek. Dove kissed her forehead. And Sadie hugged her gently, but longer than she normally might have.

Thank You for letting her be okay, Lord. Please work out the rest of this tangled mess so I don't hurt her feelings even worse. I'm so sorry.

They hugged Dutch at the door. When he squeezed Sadie around the shoulders, he tipped his head so it rested atop hers for a second or two. "Thanks for your support, Sadie. She never knew I told you, but I'll tell her now."

Sadie's sisters gaped at her while Dutch shut the door. "What was all that about?" Dove folded her arms over her chest.

Natalie stared at her. "Dutch told you…what? That Beatie was sick?"

"Sort of." Sadie walked toward their parked cars. "At Blair's wedding, that mistletoe kiss caused all sorts of problems. Dutch and Beatie didn't believe we weren't dating after that, but before we could set the record straight, Dutch confided that Beatie was undergoing medical testing. Both Mick and I had separately seen her fall, but it came as a shock to hear she'd been experiencing symptoms for a while. Anyway, Dutch said our being together brightened Beatie's spirits so much that Mick and I couldn't tell him the truth then. We decided to keep up the ruse until Beatie was more settled."

Natalie leaned against the hood of her SUV. "Why didn't you confide in us?"

"Dutch asked me and Mick not to say anything. They wanted privacy." She adjusted her fuzzy scarf, more for something to do with her hands than to ward off the chill of the fading afternoon. "I'm sorry I couldn't tell you. And I'm sorry I lied to Beatie and Dutch about dating Mick. Although, to be fair, we decided to actually date for December so it wouldn't be a total lie. We just didn't intend to continue on forever."

"I understand your wanting to make Beatie feel better during a rough time." Natalie tipped her head to the side.

"Especially since there's such a spark between you and Mick, and love makes you do dumb things sometimes."

Sadie groaned. "Don't say the *L* word."

"Why? Fake dating or no, the two of you have something."

"I do, but he doesn't." Sadie shut her eyes. "I told him I loved him after the nativity, but he reminded me we're just friends. He can never give me what I want."

"Sadie, oh, sweetheart." Dove had an arm around her in an instant. Natalie came to Sadie's other side.

As much as she appreciated her sisters' compassion, however, Sadie was about two seconds from breaking down, and she couldn't afford that today. "Thank you, and believe me, I'm going to want to cry over a gallon of ice cream with you later, but if I start now, I'll look like a blotchy tomato for Christmas Eve. And Mom will definitely notice that." Even if she didn't notice anything else about Sadie.

Natalie's eyes welled with tears. "I feel terrible for not realizing anything was off the past few days. I saw Mick's truck and assumed you were still hanging out, but he must have just been checking on Gidget."

"Same." Dove wiped a tear from her cheek with her hand.

"It's been a busy week for all of us," Sadie conceded.

"We're never too busy for you, though." Dove dug a tissue from her pocket. "Even if we missed the clues that you and Mick weren't even talking."

Speaking of missing things... Could this be an opportunity to talk to her sisters about her feelings? Part of her wanted to hold her tongue because the day was already busy, and they were standing in the street, out in the cold, but a door had just opened.

She decided to walk through it.

"Do you have another minute?"

"Sure." Dove tucked her hands into her coat pockets. "Mom doesn't arrive for another hour."

"And Wyatt's with the girls. What's up?" Natalie adjusted her position against her car.

Sadie offered a quick prayer. "We've been through so much together. Our parents arguing through our childhood. And then Dad passing away and leaving us Foxtail. I love you both, but I'm not happy."

"What do you mean?" Dove's eyes narrowed. "Did we do something?"

Yes. No. "I think I've allowed a pattern to continue, and I want to end it."

"Tell us how to help." Natalie rubbed Sadie's arm.

"It's hard to say this. It sounds almost childish. Mom would say I have classic middle-child syndrome, I suppose, but it's past time that I spoke up. Since I was young, I have felt unseen, unnoticed."

"Is this because we didn't notice you and Mick broke up?" Dove's tone wasn't accusatory. Just sad.

"No, it's lifelong. It seemed like Mom and Dad cared more about one-upping each other than paying attention to any of us, but you two received more notice than I felt like I did. You took charge at a far-too-young age, Natalie—and Dove, I think you tried to keep everyone cheerful. I'm grateful for both of those things, but as we grew up, I heard our parents praise your skills and personalities. Other kids gravitated to both of you."

"But you still feel that way?" Natalie tipped her head to the side.

"It's different, but yes. All the comments about me being single, as if I want it that way. Unless it's God's will, but that's something He and I will work out. In the meantime, I'm not happy running the farmstand, either, and I'm not sure either of you are aware of those things, because I haven't said anything. But it also seems that my circumstances have been confused with my preferences. I pray for contentment, I am grateful for what I have, but—"

It was hard to say all this. She felt petty, like a whiny kid, and empowered, like Wonder Woman, all at the same time.

Natalie squeezed her arm. "We're listening, Sadie. Tell us."

Sadie took a deep breath. "We all took on new roles to keep Foxtail in the family, but it has truncated my career as well as my personal life. Don't get me wrong, I wanted to be here in Goldenrod when Dad died. But one of the reasons I applied for the internship in Los Angeles is so I can gain skills and contacts so when our mandatory time at Foxtail ends, I can leave town and start my own shop."

Dove's jaw dropped. Natalie's eyes were wide. Then they spoke at once.

"I had no idea."

"I am so sorry, Sadie. I should have noticed these things."

"We all have a tendency to get caught up in our own lives," Sadie acknowledged. "And I should have told you both earlier. You can't read my mind."

"But we should have been better able to read *you*." Natalie shook her head. "Sometimes I haven't broached tough topics with you because I thought I was protecting you from pain. I should have comforted you instead."

"Me too." Dove leaned back. "But it ends here. Tonight, when it's quiet, let's talk about how we can help make your work at Foxtail more satisfying for the next few years until you can move on."

"Absolutely," Natalie agreed. "And the same with your personal life."

"Oh, no one can help with that." Sadie toed her boot

into the asphalt. "Mick is taking a job in Irvine just to get away from me, but let him be the one to tell Wyatt, Jillian and Gary."

"Of course. But I never thought he'd leave Goldenrod." Natalie's hand went to her mouth.

Dove seemed energized by the news, however. "There's time to talk before he goes, though. Maybe tonight?"

"I reached out to Mick earlier, but he never responded."

"What did you say in the text?" Dove bit her lip.

"It wasn't a text. I sent him flowers. Christmas roses—there's a reason for those specific flowers. Anyway, I wrote in the note that I hope he opens his heart someday because he's worthy of love. And I meant it. Even if it's not with me, I want him to be happy and fulfilled."

Dove's chin trembled. "I want that for you, too, Sadie. I'm sorry for the ways I made you feel less than, especially with my little comments about you not dating. I was insensitive."

"Thank you." Sadie hugged her before moving on to Natalie. "You two are the best sisters anyone could ask for."

"Hey, that's my line." Natalie wiped a tear from her cheek. Then she pulled her buzzing phone from her pocket. "It's Wyatt. He said Mick will be here shortly, and he'd like to pop by then too."

"I'd rather not be here when he arrives." Sadie unlocked the minivan. "I have to make a casserole for tonight, anyway."

"Why don't you get changed and then come make it at my house? You too, Dove. We can have a good solid chat and bake cookies. We haven't done that together in so long. And then when Mom arrives, we'll all be there to welcome her."

"Sounds nice." And distracting, so she wouldn't mope over Mick as much as if she were alone.

Dove never said no to baking. "We can serve the cookies at the party."

Sadie recalled that tonight would have been her and Mick's twelfth date of Christmas…the party, then the church service, her favorite of the year. She had been so looking forward to sitting together in the pew. And then driving around to look at Christmas lights.

But that wasn't happening, and it was time to focus on Christmas itself. The gift of God in His Son, Jesus—the greatest gift Sadie would ever receive.

She was grateful for the gift from her sisters this year too. Not whatever presents they had purchased and placed beneath the tree, but their loving support and the newfound sense of unity she sensed between them all.

Lord, will Mick and I someday be able to return to a place of peace and reconciliation too?

Sadie prayed they would, with all her heart.

Sadie couldn't have imagined a merrier Christmas Eve party.

Festive carols played over the sound system at Wyatt and Natalie's house while the delectable aromas of pine, vanilla-laced cookies and honey-baked ham spiced the air. The tree lights twinkled while guests wearing holiday sweaters bustled between the rooms, chatting.

Sadie, dressed for the occasion in her velvety green pants with a soft cream sweater, carried a tray of empty cider mugs past Gary and Thatcher while they talked horses—something they had in common.

She slipped into the kitchen, which was abuzz with activity. Wyatt sliced the ham, Dove removed yeast rolls from the oven, Jillian spooned glaze into a gravy bowl, Natalie tossed a salad and their mom, Yvonne, dropped a cube of butter atop a bowl of steaming-hot mashed potatoes.

"Such a shame about Beatie and Dutch having to miss the party," Mom was saying as Sadie tucked the empty mugs in the dishwasher. "I haven't seen Mick yet either. Did he have a pet emergency or something?"

"Something came up, yes." Jillian cast an apologetic glance at Sadie.

Sadie hated that Mick was missing Christmas Eve with his family to avoid her. She was sure her face reflected her jumbled emotions, so she took the bowl of potatoes and the gravy boat. "I'll set these on the buffet."

After that, she started to return to the kitchen, but she decided to take a moment to get her emotions in check. The only empty room was the office, which was dark and quiet.

She perched at the window and saw the tiniest snowflakes floating down from the sky. Not enough snow would accumulate to sled in, although little Rose and Luna might enjoy stomping around outside tomorrow in their bright pink boots.

"Ant Zadie?"

Sadie turned around to find Rose, precious in a scarlet dress, toddling up to her, hands extended. How fast she and Luna had grown. Two and half years old already, and such sweethearts. Sadie scooped her up in her arms.

"Have you been having fun with your sister and Juniper and Miss Bliss?" Bliss and her foster daughter had brought the twins sticker books, and they had been playing with them in front of the Christmas tree when Sadie had passed by to reach the office.

Rose played with the decorative buttons along Sadie's shoulder. "I wanna say some-fin' to you."

"Yes, my love?"

"It's Cwismas," Rose announced.

"It sure is. After dinner we'll go to church to thank God for Jesus, and then tomorrow—"

The doorbell's abrupt ring made her jump. "I'll get it," she called as she strode out of the office. "Or rather, we will, won't we, Rose? Let's see who it is."

She opened the door wide to a smiling Dutch and Beatie.

"What a wonderful surprise. Please, come in."

"Is it all right if our friend joins us?"

Friend? But there was no one else there.

"Horsie." Rosie pointed down with a wet finger.

Sadie's gaze dropped. Gidget stood at Beatie's knee, wearing a red service animal vest.

Natalie ushered them inside, letting out a brief squeal. "Does this mean what I think it means?"

"Mick came by after you left, and we talked about Gidget living with us," Dutch said as he shrugged out of his jacket. "It turns out she's a good fit for Beatie's visual impairments and balance issues."

"A perfect fit," Sadie agreed.

"I already knew she was perfect," Beatie gushed, giving the little horse a pat. "I never met a sweeter creature. So Mick went and got her for me."

Sadie had never seen his truck at Foxtail, but then again, she hadn't been in the farmstand since noon.

"What's this?" Thatcher joined them in the foyer. "A new family member?"

The others welcomed the three arrivals with joy and affection, fawning over Beatie and Gidget.

"Just in time to eat." Wyatt shook Dutch's hand and then offered his arm to Beatie. "May I escort you to the table?"

"Yes, please."

Beatie took a seat on a padded chair at the dining room

table with house-trained Gidget staying at her side. Sadie buckled Rose in her high chair beside Luna's. Unlike at Thanksgiving, all the guests couldn't fit around one table. Food would be served buffet-style, and guests could eat anywhere they found space. Sadie planned to sit on the fireplace hearth if it was free.

She was snapping Rose's bib around her neck when the front door shut loudly. She looked up to see Mick striding into the dining room, a teasing grin on his face and a dusting of snow on his shoulders and hair. There was a noticeable lack of stubble on his jaw or chin, testifying that he had recently shaved, and he wore a navy-blue sweater with a rolled collar that made his eyes pop.

She was so captivated, so stunned at him being here, looking *happy* of all things, that she was startled when Fly jogged past her to join Wyatt's dog, Ranger, in the corner with a toy.

Her heart flew into a gallop. *Lord, help me get through this with no drama.* She had to do her best because she and Mick would forever be bound by Wyatt and Natalie, Rose and Luna.

Forever was a long time to feel his rejection.

She had been so foolish to let herself fall for him. Although, to be honest, she wasn't sure she could've stopped it if she had tried. Mick filled the room with his presence, and not just because of his height and strength. He was a man who matched people with animals, who brought Christmas roses to the manger at the living nativity—

Good gumdrops, he had pinned a Christmas rose to his sweater. One of the blooms from the bouquet she'd sent.

What on earth is happening, Lord?

Mick, meanwhile, was making the rounds. Wyatt clapped

his shoulder. "I didn't hear you come in, but I'm glad you made it." Something like an apology passed between them.

"I thought you weren't coming at all." Jillian stood, smiling.

"Unka Mick!" Luna yelled from the highchair.

"Hi, squirt." He chucked her cheek, then did the same to Rose.

Natalie glanced at Sadie, but forced a smile for him. "Grab a plate, Mick."

"Thanks, but I want to give Sadie her Christmas present before I eat."

The room fell silent, except for the holiday music and the dogs' wet munching on their toys.

"We don't exchange presents," Sadie blurted.

"Sure, we do. You sent me flowers."

"She did?" Beatie's whisper wasn't as subtle as she'd probably intended.

"I'm so confused right now," Mom muttered. "What's going on?"

"Shh." Dutch cupped his ear.

Sadie was blushing so hot she was probably as red as the stripes on a candy cane, but Mick looked cool and collected as he met her gaze. "My gift for you is outside, if you want to come with me."

"Why do you have to go outside to see it? Is it a car?" Thatcher joked.

Dove lightly smacked his arm, and Natalie glared at him.

"Let's go," she said. The silence followed Sadie and Mick from the room.

She pulled her coat from the rack in the foyer and stepped out onto the porch, all decorated with garland and twinkling white lights. When Mick shut the front door behind him, she turned around to face him, noting damp spots from melted snowflakes on his shoulders. "Didn't you wear a jacket?"

"I left it in the car. I didn't want to crush my rose." He tipped his head to the left, the side where he'd attached the flower to his sweater with a safety pin. "I didn't do a great job of making it into a boutonniere."

It might not sell in a store, no, but it was the most beautiful thing in the world to her because it was a gesture of goodwill. "It's perfect. I'm glad you received the bouquet. Elena dropped it off on your porch just after noon."

"I didn't get home until half an hour ago." He leaned against the porch railing, his eyes dark blue in the purple-pink glow of the setting winter sun. "I stayed late at the clinic, and then I visited my aunt, and then I went to Beatie's, and—did you see Gidget tonight?" He looked so excited that it was impossible not to smile.

"I did. That was a brilliant idea, pairing them up. Beatie will have some challenges in the future, but she'll be able to face them with more confidence with Gidget at her side."

"They'll make a great team. Just like us, Sadie."

Relief flooded her, calming her pattering heart. "Judging by you wearing the flower, it seems like you're willing for us to be friends again. And that's the most wonderful gift you could give me, Mick, thank you."

"That isn't the gift—not like that, anyway." He moved to stand in front of her, close enough for her to see his pulse beating at the tender spot on his neck. "It's a promise to be honest with you…and myself. I realize now how much I've been lying to myself about my feelings. And then I told the same lies to you, saying that I can't love you. But I already did love you, and I will my until heart stops beating."

Sadie forgot how to breathe. "What?"

"My heart is yours, Sadie, now and always. If you don't

want it, I'd understand, but I pray you can forgive me, even though I don't deserve it. The things I said, and the way I left you on the path?" His stricken gaze searched her face. "I'm so sorry."

Mick had been so hurt, so rejected, in his life. Opening himself like this was an act of bravery, and she couldn't help thinking of the story of the Christmas rose. That one's heart was the best gift of all.

But her eyes stung with tears as she shook her head. "I forgive you, and I love you, but you don't have to do this. It's not what you wanted at all."

"Hey, sweetheart, shh." He cupped her cheeks in his hands and swiped her tears with his thumbs. "It *is* what I wanted, but I've been too big of a fool to realize it. I never allowed myself to think about why we were such close friends or how deep our relationship went because I didn't want to get hurt. In fact, I let my heart petrify to stone in my chest because that's what I thought it took to protect it. But there's still life in it, and I see now that we've been on this path for a long time. Best friends to love."

She placed her hands atop his. "Are you sure?"

He nodded. "But I'm scared to death. I know that doesn't sound macho, but you terrify me, Sadie Dalton."

"I'm not scary. I'm just Sadie." Her hands slipped down to wrap around his warm waist. "And I'm not going anywhere."

"Yes, you are. Los Angeles next week. But I'll be here when you come back."

"What about the job in Irvine?"

"I'm going to pass on it. Leonard forgot something at the clinic and found my resignation letter on his desk. He was so upset, he called, and after I took Gidget to Beatie, we met for coffee and a good talk. He agreed to make some changes so my grandpa's clinic can better serve animals and people.

It won't all happen overnight, but I'll be content. Talking to my aunt about our relationship clarified some things to me about patience—"

"Wait, you talked to your aunt?"

"Yes, and I'll fill you in later. It's all good, I promise. She said…" He swallowed hard. "She loves me."

"Oh, Mick." Her heart flooded with gratitude. "That's wonderful." And long overdue.

"I also talked to Wyatt a little, to fill him in and make things better between us. Right now, though, I want to talk about you." His smile was bright as the Christmas star. "Like I said, I'll be here when you get back from LA, and when your time at Foxtail is up, I will go with you. I grew up in Goldenrod, but I never felt rooted until I realized you were the reason why. You are my home."

His words sent a thrill through her. "And you are mine, but I'm not going anywhere, Mick. I—we are staying in Goldenrod."

His brow furrowed. "You can't do what you love here, and there's no way I'm going to keep that from you."

"You aren't the only one who had a life-altering talk today. My sisters and I—well, we're on a road to a better place, too, and for the past few hours we've been baking cookies and figuring out where to build a flower shop on the Foxtail property once we're clear of the terms of Dad's will. Right now, we can't add to the business, as you know, but in a few years? I'm going to have a floral-design shop kitty-corner to the bakery."

"That's wonderful, but are you sure it's the best idea? You really wanted to start fresh, and you had concerns about competition in town with Goldenrod Floral Design."

"True, and it might be a slow start, but…" Where to

begin?" "Remember the near catastrophe with the five hundred poinsettias last week?"

"I doubt I'll ever forget."

"Me, either, but not because of the panic I felt when they were dropped off in front of the farmstand. I keep thinking about how much I loved turning them into a fundraiser."

Mick's smile softened. "It was an inspired idea, and you handled it so well. The way you stood up to speak at the shelter party? You were charming."

"I don't know about that, but this past month, I've learned so much about myself—as a person uniquely crafted by God. I talked to Kelsey about the gifts God gave her, but I never looked at myself with that sort of consideration until recently. I recognized that I truly enjoyed preparing the poinsettias for the fundraiser. And another thing I love is repurposing leftover flowers and vases to give away."

"I remember talking about that. You do such a good job."

"But what if I could do more? When I was talking to my sisters, I realized that if I had more space—say, in my own flower shop—I could easily store used vases, picks and supplies to craft new arrangements from extra flowers, and then donate to the nursing home, veterans' groups or the hospital."

"This is amazing, Sadie, but you could do that anywhere. I want you to be sure you want to stay here."

"Flowers are more to me than a way to make a living. They add beauty and joy to life, and there are so many people going through difficult times who could use a smile. I want Foxtail Floral Design to give back to the community, and I don't know if I could engage in the same ways if I lived in a bigger town."

"Then it sounds like we're both staying in Goldenrod." He brushed a lock of hair from her temple. "I love you,

Sadie. For your bright ideas and gifts and talents, your beautiful eyes and open heart. I love you. Those aren't the easiest words to say, growing up the way I did, but I mean them. With all that I am, I love you."

She knew how hard it was for him to give voice to his feelings, and she cherished the gift. She had no such difficulty, however. "I love you, Mick, and I will remind you every day for the rest of my life."

She might have said more, but he bent his head and kissed her, slow at first, but then deeper, and she forgot everything but him and how protected and cherished he made her feel.

When he pulled away, Sadie snuggled into his chest, relishing the moment. His chin rested atop her head, and then, soft as a breath, he whispered. "Fox."

Slowly, she turned her head. Sure enough, a gray and brown animal the size of a bulldog watched them from beneath an oak. Then it dashed into the bushes with the rustle of leaves.

"I haven't seen one since November." Sadie returned her cheek to his chest. "The same day you agreed to be my date to Blair's wedding."

"Best decision I ever made." His arms fell, but he never broke contact as his fingers traced her arms down to take hold of both her hands. "I thought I was doing a favor for my closest friend, but God had much grander things in mind. Reconciliation with my family. Teaching me that I wasn't so broken that He couldn't heal me. Showing me one of His greatest gifts was right in front of me all along."

She was so overcome by his words that she didn't register that he was moving until he was kneeling before her, pulling something from his jacket pocket. "Sadie Noel Dalton. The person who loved me enough to help me love again.

My beautiful girl, my best friend, my heart. Will you do me the honor of becoming my wife?"

He opened the box, revealing a solitaire diamond on a classic gold band. "Yes, Mick. I love you so much. But when did you find a ring?"

"This is my mother's, but if you don't like it, we can look for another. I didn't want to wait, though. We may not have ever *really* dated—"

"I want to marry my best friend. And this is the most beautiful ring I've ever seen. Knowing it belonged to your mother makes it even more meaningful."

Her hands trembled as he slipped the ring onto the fourth finger of her left hand, and then he was on his feet, kissing her tenderly.

His lips trailed to her hairline. "When do you want to get married? Best Friends Day, maybe?"

She laughed, remembering that morning last month when he had parked the clinic's old trailer at the farmstand. "I would marry you tomorrow, but I can't leave Foxtail for another few years."

"Then we'll live at Foxtail." He kissed the top of her head. "In your apartment or in a trailer in the orchard. I don't care, as long as I'm with you."

"That's all I want too. So much that even though I hate to go back inside the house, I'm excited to tell everyone we're engaged. And to have a little talk with Dutch and Beatie."

"True. As much as I'd prefer a little more time alone with you, we have another fifty or sixty years for this."

Her lips pulled up in a sly grin. "One question. Am I going to have to give up marshmallows? Because I'm not sure I can go without them in my cocoa for the rest of my life."

The playful growl in his throat made her giggle, but when he kissed her again, she became 100 percent serious.

Snuggling into him afterward, she sighed in contentment. "Forget the marshmallows. I choose this."

He seemed to like her answer, the way he held her tighter. "You can fill our house with as many marshmallows as you want, honey."

"Nah, I'm good." She would never miss them. Her life was already sweet enough as it was.

* * * * *

If you liked this story from Susanne Dietze,
check out her previous Love Inspired books:

Mountain Homecoming
The Secret Between Them
A Need to Protect

Available now from Love Inspired!
Find more great reads at www.LoveInspired.com.

Dear Reader,

Welcome back to Foxtail Farm! I hope you enjoyed Sadie and Mick's journey to love, healing and reconciliation. Personally, I love the "friends to more" trope because the couple's relationship is already built on a solid foundation of trust, compatibility and, in Sadie and Mick's case, a lot of inside jokes! I also enjoy it when a character realizes the person they've come to love (or loved all along) is already the one who knew them best.

Being loved and known, together, is a core human need that God meets in His care for us. This holiday season, I pray that your celebrations are rich in the knowledge that Jesus knows and loves you so much that He came that first Christmas to offer His life for you and for me. Joy to the world! The Lord is come!

I love to chat with readers, and you can find me on my website, www.SusanneDietze.com.

Merry Christmas!
Susanne Dietze

Get up to 4 Free Books!

We'll send you 2 free books from each series you try PLUS a free Mystery Gift.

FREE Value Over **$25**

Both the **Love Inspired®** and **Love Inspired® Suspense** series feature compelling novels filled with inspirational romance, faith, forgiveness and hope.

YES! Please send me 2 FREE novels from the Love Inspired or Love Inspired Suspense series and my FREE gift (gift is worth about $10 retail). After receiving them, if I don't wish to receive any more books, I can return the shipping statement marked "cancel." If I don't cancel, I will receive 6 brand-new Love Inspired Larger-Print books or Love Inspired Suspense Larger-Print books every month and be billed just $7.19 each in the U.S. or $7.99 each in Canada. That is a savings of 20% off the cover price. It's quite a bargain! Shipping and handling is just 50¢ per book in the U.S. and $1.25 per book in Canada.* I understand that accepting the 2 free books and gift places me under no obligation to buy anything. I can always return a shipment and cancel at any time by calling the number below. The free books and gift are mine to keep no matter what I decide.

Choose one:
- ☐ **Love Inspired Larger-Print** (122/322 BPA G36Y)
- ☐ **Love Inspired Suspense Larger-Print** (107/307 BPA G36Y)
- ☐ **Or Try Both!** (122/322 & 107/307 BPA G36Z)

Name (please print)

Address _____ Apt. #

City _____ State/Province _____ Zip/Postal Code

Email: Please check this box ☐ if you would like to receive newsletters and promotional emails from Harlequin Enterprises ULC and its affiliates. You can unsubscribe anytime.

> **Mail to the Harlequin Reader Service:**
> **IN U.S.A.:** P.O. Box 1341, Buffalo, NY 14240-8531
> **IN CANADA:** P.O. Box 603, Fort Erie, Ontario L2A 5X3

Want to explore our other series or interested in ebooks? Visit www.ReaderService.com or call 1-800-873-8635.

---

*Terms and prices subject to change without notice. Prices do not include sales taxes, which will be charged (if applicable) based on your state or country of residence. Canadian residents will be charged applicable taxes. Offer not valid in Quebec. This offer is limited to one order per household. Books received may not be as shown. Not valid for current subscribers to the Love Inspired or Love Inspired Suspense series. All orders subject to approval. Credit or debit balances in a customer's account(s) may be offset by any other outstanding balance owed by or to the customer. Please allow 4 to 6 weeks for delivery. Offer available while quantities last.

Your Privacy—Your information is being collected by Harlequin Enterprises ULC, operating as Harlequin Reader Service. For a complete summary of the information we collect, how we use this information and to whom it is disclosed, please visit our privacy notice located at https://corporate.harlequin.com/privacy-notice. Notice to California Residents – Under California law, you have specific rights to control and access your data. For more information on these rights and how to exercise them, visit https://corporate.harlequin.com/california-privacy. For additional information for residents of other U.S. states that provide their residents with certain rights with respect to personal data, visit https://corporate.harlequin.com/other-state-residents-privacy-rights/.

LIRLIS25